Pride Publishing books by Bailey Bradford

What Matters Most
Ex's and O's
A Bit of Me
A Bit of You
In My Arms Tonight
Where There's a Will
My Heart to Keep

Leopard's Spots
Levi
Oscar
Timothy
Isaiah
Gilbert
Esau
Sullivan
Wesley
Nischal
Justice
Sabin
Cliff

Mossy Glenn Ranch
Chaps and Hope
Ropes and Dreams
Saddles and Memories
Fences and Freedom
Riding and Regrets
Broncs and Bullies
Hay and Heartbreak
Vaqueros and Vigilance

Spotless
Hide
Hunt
Home
Heart

Mystic Tattoos
One Too Many

Valen's Pack
Run with the Moon
Exodus

The Vamp for Me
My Life Without Garlic
Don't Stake My Life on It
Sunshine is Overrated
Don't Drink the Holy Water
The Trouble with Mirrors
That's One Cross Vamp

Calendar Men
Mr. January
Mr. February
Mr. March
Mr. April
Mr. May
Mr. June
Mr. July
Mr. August
Mr September
Mr. October
Mr. November
Mr. December
The 13th Month

Coyote's Call
Off Course
In from the Cold
Blue Moon Rising

Power
Exchange
Submit
Dominate

Hooked on You
In Deep

Intrinsic Values
Artifacts
Antiques

City Shifters
Bearly There
Harey Situation

Wild Ones
Destined Prey
Destined Predator
Destined Prize

Fire and Flutter
Dragon Dreams and Fairy Wings
Wyvern Ways and Elven Magic
Griffin Days and Pixe Nights

Triple Threat
Howling for More

Anthologies
What's his Passion?: Unexpected Places
What's his Passion?: Unexpected Moments
Racing Hearts: The Lonely Ones

Fire & Flutter

GRIFFIN DAYS AND PIXIE NIGHTS

BAILEY BRADFORD

Griffin Days and Pixie Nights
ISBN # 978-1-80250-505-4
©Copyright Bailey Bradford 2023
Cover Art by Erin Dameron-Hill ©Copyright January 2023
Interior text design by Claire Siemaszkiewicz
Pride Publishing

GRIFFIN DAYS AND PIXIE NIGHTS

Dedication

To whoever needs to hear this — you are a miracle.

Chapter One

"Sir!" The guard on duty outside the two-room suite in the Griffin Guardians HQ sprang to attention at Captain Gage's approach. He snapped out a smart salute, but his hand fell when Gage didn't march past but instead stood waiting in the corridor. "Sir...?" he repeated, uncertainly.

"As you were." Gage jerked his head to one side, illustrating how he wanted the corporal — returned to his position in between the doors and not in front of one of them.

The guard took a quick glance at the sheet of parchment paper pinned to the board on the wall. "Captain, you're not listed as — "

"Stand aside, *Corporal*." Gage added a raised eyebrow to the emphasis he placed on the last word and the junior officer recoiled.

Some officers might have raised their voice, or tapped their uniform badges, drawing the corporal's attention to the greater number of feathers displayed.

That would have reminded the junior who was of a higher rank in the Griffin Guardians, the kingdom's elite federal law enforcement agency that griffin shifters ran and dedicated their lives to.

Gage never wanted or needed to pull rank, either here inside the HQ or outside. His height and breadth, coupled with his implacable, unflinching manner did it for him. Now was no different — the corporal not only scuttled to one side, but opened the door for him and saluted again. Gage murmured his thanks. While he liked how the junior officer had assessed and regrouped, he didn't like that a situation demanding such a response existed.

The list displayed outside in the corridor was a symbol of all that was going the wrong way in the Guardians, in Gage's opinion. This bureaucratic keeping account of which griffin shifter was assigned to which aspect of which case in which room at which time was getting out of claw.

What had Colm said last week? *"Pretty soon admin will be assigning us times for bathroom breaks, and probably make us sign in and out of the stall if we take a dump."* It had been a joke, but Gage hadn't laughed. Not many of them had.

The two first lieutenants on duty in the observation room sprang to their feet, shooting puzzled looks at each other when Gage marched in, but both sat when Gage waved them down.

"Don't worry. I'm not here to supervise how you're implementing some new directive that came into force five minutes ago or check if you're reaching your latest performance targets," he told them, trying to sound lighter than he felt.

He made straight for the mirror-pane that divided this small room from the equally small but brighter room beyond.

It was a light-mirror, meaning that he couldn't use it to see his reflection, but he wasn't there to do that. He knew his uniform would be clean and crisp — Guardians' uniforms were designed that way — just as his blond hair, short back and sides and longer on top, was regulation length and cut. He bet his face bore the same narrow-eyed, focused look it always did. What he wanted was to look through the light-mirror to its other side.

But what he didn't expect was that the moment his gaze found the prisoner in the interrogation room, the prisoner would raise his head and stare back at him through the glass.

"The hells?" First Lieutenant Antonin exclaimed. His chair scraped on the floor behind him as he joined Gage. "He can't see through the glass?"

"He's a *mage*," Gage reminded his fellow officers, spitting the words out. "Who knows what these magic users can do?" His revulsion left a sour taste in his mouth as he continued, "His powers have been dampened, yes?"

"As much as the regs allow, Sir." First Lieutenant Sandrine joined them at the mirror, giving a choked-off exclamation when the prisoner sent a mocking finger-wave her way.

Gage swore. "This tricky bastard needs neutralizing, stat."

"I'm afraid we can't, Sir. Not until the request's been approved and stamped by two duty officers and the prisoner's been examined and cleared by the HQ physician." Antonin tucked his chair back into the table.

"New regulations, Sir," Sandrine added.

Both Antonin and Sandrine sounded apologetic, but it wasn't their fault, nor were they telling Gage anything he didn't know. Neither of those things made the information easier to hear, or the situation any easier to bear, however. Gage's hand had formed into a fist, and he exhaled as he opened it flat again, wishing he could huff away all the irritation and frustration he was feeling as easily.

Few people could say, their hand on their heart, that they loved their job, and Gage would never say that either, because being a Griffin Guardian was more than a job to him. The corps was his life, and he took pride in the knowledge that he'd given the organization his all since joining the Guardians thirty years ago. *That's good...isn't it? Laudable?* Because lately he'd begun to feel that, well, perhaps it wasn't.

He hauled in those stray thoughts. If he was feeling that there could perhaps be more to his life, it was because every moon-cycle seemed to bring with it new guidelines and directives, most of them aimed at giving what Gage still thought of as the lesser beings 'representation' or 'a voice' and making sure the higher beings — sorry, winged beings — didn't abuse what was becoming increasingly seen as their position of privilege.

Gage wasn't political or even very aware of interspecies politics. All he knew was that the new social climate made it increasingly hard for him to perform his duties, thanks to the 'accountability' and 'visibility' and every other hells-be-damned 'ility' the Equality Awareness Office dreamed up, and hamstrung the entire corps with, from its five-feathered general down to its lowliest private.

"Rules are one thing," he muttered. He liked rules. Lived by rules. Wished all the species did, that they followed the same ones as the griffin kingdom did. The griffins' codes of conduct and honor were revered throughout the plane, as was their ability to impose order, making them the natural choice for a federal law enforcement species. *A mission undertaken is a mission accomplished.* It was no coincidence that this was the Guardians' motto. "Rules keep things safe."

"I'm so sorry about Captain Colm, Sir," Sandrine said, perhaps catching Gage's last words.

Gage gave her a brusque nod in acknowledgment. He was sorry too. He'd had Colm as partner for the last ten years of his three decades in the Griffin Guardians, and they worked together well. Colm was as reliable and committed to getting the job done as Gage could want. There were always risks, in the job they did, of course, but to think that that contemptuous bastard sitting there—

"It was an accident. And I have no idea why he was chasing me. Why either of them were, these winged shifter beasts, whatever they were. Dragons, right?"

The mage's voice held defiance and there was triumph in the gaze he leveled at Gage through the glass as he spoke. But when he added a derisive kiss to the end of his sentence, Gage was out of the observation room and into the one next door almost before he was aware of moving or that he'd had all he could take. He had an assignment and he would do what it took to see it through. That was the way he operated. How he saw the world.

"Out," he ordered the second lieutenant in the interrogation room before the officer had gotten out the S of *Sir*. "Now!" he snapped. He rounded on the prisoner the second the door was closed, his eyes narrowed. "So. It's just you and me now, scum."

"I'm a *mage*," the prisoner snarked. "Which means that I'm — "

"Oh, excuse me. *Mage* scum," Gage snapped. "A mage scum con artist who used his 'magic' to rob money-vaults and businesses, having found a way around the thief protections. One who I came to question, which, for the record, is why you tried to run, and in your escape, you injured my partner." He let the fury he felt show.

"What? I did that? Well, that was wrong of me. I made a mistake there." The mage looked down at the desk in front of him for a few seconds. When he looked up again, his eyes grew darker as he turned his head slowly toward Gage. By the time he stared full force at him, his eyes were completely black, with no white to them at all. The effect was unnerving and the revealed strength of his powers worrying. Gage braced himself.

"Because I was aiming for the both of you." The mage got to his feet, his movements swift and jerky. Snakelike, almost. "You're stronger than your partner, though. Colm, wasn't it? Or isn't it, if he's still alive? Pity. A two-for-one hit-and-destroy would have saved me time and effort."

"Like you've saved us time and effort?" Gage kept his voice quiet when he wanted to yell at this piece of troll shit. "By confessing?" He smirked.

"Oh, if only anyone had witnessed it, either visually or audibly." The mage pulled a pitying face. "If only the mirror-glass hadn't silvered, and the listening holes hadn't all blocked." He gave Gage time to take in his meaning.

What — ? Gage took his eyes off the prisoner to throw a glance at the light-mirror and the conduit holes below it.

"Because without a record of this, it's like I was never here, griffin. And that being the case, I think I'll be off." The mage moved.

Instantly, Gage took a step forward to block him. "Oh, we just let you walk out of here, do we?" he scoffed.

The mage shrugged, as if he didn't care, then brought his hands up at lightning speed and weaved his fingers in a quick, complex pattern. "A state of balance or a lack of motion," he began, his voice low, and his eyes glowing a molten silver. Before Gage understood or could make him cease, he continued, his volume getting louder with each word, "A slowing or stoppage of a *flow*."

He brought his hands together on the last word, the clap loud, and the stasis spell he'd cast hit Gage like a punch to the stomach. It didn't have him staggering backward or knock him onto his ass like a physical blow would, though. Instead, it trapped him in place, unable to move. With a caw of triumph, the prisoner thumbed his nose at Gage, opened the door and walked out.

No. No no no! We should have neutered him, regulations be damned! Gage heaved in a breath, fighting with all his strength. That troll-dung mage had said Gage was stronger than his partner, which was true, but not true enough. Gage was stronger than any Griffin Guardian currently in the corps or in its records. He trained and honed the strength and resistance in his muscles and sinews and mind and spirit, increasing year-on-year what he could battle — and defeat.

Fighting the spell cast on him was like pulling himself along a too-narrow corridor whose walls were lined with broken glass, but he ignored the jagged shards ripping into him and actually — he saw, glancing down — rending his uniform and cutting his flesh. The pain barely registered and any spots of blood staining the gray tunic and pants vanished, just as rips in the fabric disappeared.

With one final almighty heave Gage was free. Panting, he shook off the remains of the stasis bind to hurl himself to the door. The mage was at the end of the corridor by now, and there was enough of his residual power left dusted on Gage for Gage to see the outline of the shield spell the prisoner had cloaked himself in.

The pull of the magic used snapped from its victim to its caster, the rogue mage who stopped in his tracks and turned around. The drop of the prisoner's jaw on seeing Gage free was the only amusing thing about the situation. The mage whipped around again and broke into a run.

"Stop!" Gage yelled, and the command in his voice had everyone freezing…everyone except the one he wanted to, the one who was making for the large window at the end of the corridor.

The mage ran faster, gathering speed and power. If that didn't give a hint about his escape plan, the hissed incantation and his hand outstretched toward the window did. A crack and the glass was gone. It hadn't shattered, but vanished, leaving the window frame gaping empty. The mage had already demonstrated an affinity with glass, but Gage had no intention of letting the bastard use it as an exit route. He sped up too.

"Captain, you can't!" Second Lieutenant Ralnd yelled behind him.

Oh, but Gage could. This was his case and he was doing whatever it took to close it.

Whatever it took.

Chapter Two

"Come close, come close! Don't be shy there!" Daire the pixie took one hand off the pfeife he was playing and beckoned the trickle of crowd nearer. Calculating how many of them were out-of-towners, he resumed his tune, holding the small woodwind instrument across his mouth to make it trill and sing.

He liked the thready, breathy sound of a pfeife and how quickly it gathered people, swaying and clapping along to the music...and generally distracted.

He wasn't the best player ever, but the tiniest hint of compulsion he'd puffed over himself helped. It made the music more compelling, put a brighter twinkle in his glass-green eyes and gave a shinier gleam to his wavy chestnut-brown hair. He shook his shoulder-length locks back, revealing his pointed ears, which got their own gasp from those of his audience who'd never been this close to a pixie before.

Daire wished he could enhance things more, but he'd had to use the smallest charm he could get away with...without attracting attention. Well, the wrong kind of attention. He didn't have a license to make music for a crowd, for one thing, and would never be granted one, for another. Authority tended to be as suspicious of him as he was disdainful of it.

"That music is *spellbinding*," sighed a blonde woman listening. She blushed when Daire winked at her.

Today's marks were here in the capital for some event or other, Daire supposed. *Good.* He stamped a foot, thickening the compulsion to the point he could safely work a second charm. He wasn't the best spellcaster either, but he made out all right. Usually. His enchantments didn't tend to last that long, reflecting the level of effort he put in — low — the degree of study he went in for — minimal — and the quality of the raw ingredients he used — the lowest that would function.

Well, the price of herb and roots these days. He wasn't a brownie, grubbing around in the dirt for what he needed, so had no choice but to pixie up the gelt for it, but tried to keep costs low. *Or nonexistent.*

The echo charm he used now trapped his image and sound, so that to onlookers, he still stood against the wall near the marketplace, small and slim, one foot bent up behind him to rest on the white stone, his arched red-brown eyebrows and uptilted nose denoting his species just as much as the color of his eyes or the tips of his ears did.

He didn't quite have the length and slimness of fingers considered 'pure' pixie, but his were good enough…to pickpocket the crowd he now wandered among, relieving purses and coin-bags of their contents. Small items in pockets that caught his curiosity were lifted out too. Oh, the blonde, at whom he'd winked, carried a tube of red luststick, that aphrodisiac for lips, did she? One kiss from her and a guy — or gal — wouldn't just be back for more. He or she wouldn't go away.

Best of luck to her. He just hoped she used it sparingly. At least he had no need to remind himself not to pucker up for her, not when his tastes ran a lot taller, broader and shorter-haired. He tried his luck with the fatter woman next to the blonde one and — *Shit!*

He bit back a screech just in time at the rawdent that he'd disturbed in her bag and that had now emerged, clinging to his finger — by its teeth. *A pocket shrew? Who totes one of those around?* They were the worst. Gods, they weren't the new purse pet, were they? That could crimp his plans. He'd almost prefer that caterwauls made a comeback. He finally shook the savage furball off him and moved on quickly, because it looked like it was getting ready to try his ankle next.

Hm, what does this rather rough-looking gent have tucked away here? Something small and round, but not a coin. Daire's imagination boggled, coming up with everything from a magic wishing stone to a gold piece that returned to the spender after each use. A pixie could dream...

Daire eased the item free of the man's fanny-pack, reflecting that the mark was one of life's born victims, if he wore one of those. When he saw what the wooden token was, Daire risked breaking his spell by exclaiming out loud. A pass to enter the dog-racing tracks!

"You little beauty," Daire breathed. He raised the pass to his lips and kissed it, tears in his eyes. *Sainted stars and holy heavens, this is my lucky day!*

Or so he hoped. He must be due for some, surely? He wasn't a betting addict. More of an enthusiast. It wasn't like he had a gambling problem. More a losing problem, just lately. It happened, to the sort of pixie who couldn't pass an oddsmaker's without going in, or one who'd take any bet going. But this — it was a sign that he should get himself to the races!

He dashed back and dived into his image, managing not to squeal at the resistance he had to pass through, like breaking the surface of icy water. Taking over, or retaking his place, he brought his tune to a loud, shrill roll of completion.

"Well, how about applauding?" he demanded into the silence that hung thick in the square once his reedy notes died away. "Wouldn't kill you now, would it?" Grinning, he snatched up his floppy hat from the ground before anyone went to look for coins to throw in it. Shouting, "I'll be back at sundown, people!" he clapped the hat on and ran to the tracks.

There, he enjoyed so much brandishing his pass to barge through the gate instead of waiting in line and handing over coins, or in his case, trying to talk his way in. One of the security giants bit into his pass to check it.

"Careful, you'll get splinters," Daire warned, snatching the token back. Inside, he turned sharply away from the gate and rubbed his hands in glee, taking a minute to drink in the sights, sounds and scents he loved before looking for the listing of which wind-hounds were running in the two o'clock.

He eased through the crowds, sniffing the fried food and stopping for a fish cracker, but wrinkling his nose at the beaver tails in the kiosk next door. Most pixies loved that delicacy, but Daire thought it a little much to cut the rawdents' tails off and fry them, even if the beavers did grow a new one every month.

He reached out to slap Lyam on the back when he passed the spelt-wheat-beer tent. His greeting startled Lyam, making him slop beer from a tankard onto the customer he was serving. The customer leapt up and yelled, clouting poor Lyam around the head.

"Sorry!" Daire called over his shoulder. He couldn't stop and try to get a beer when the owner wasn't looking, not when he had to find an oddsmaker who'd let him bet. Fine, he'd admit he had a fondness for games of chance. Not a *weakness*. He wouldn't go that far. Ooh, Oddsmaker Aldon was right there, with a group of Daire's friends clustered around his chalk board. Daire shook his head again at the track accountant's slogan — *You're All Done With Aldon*. It was one of the worst.

"Daire?" Clove caught sight of him and laughed. "Who let you in?"

"I have a pass, actually." Daire flicked it into the air and caught it. Quickly. He couldn't be too careful with the types who frequented this place. "So stick that up your pixie pipe and pass it."

"Best offer he's had all day," Brackish said of Clove, slapping him on the shoulder.

Clove slapped him back. Harder. "Got a lead on an invisibility stone," he told Daire. "You interested?"

Daire considered. He did like getting his hands on amulets and charms, and Clove had sold him a few things over the years. "Maybe," he replied. "If it works better than that so-called love potion."

"That worked!" Clove protested.

"Yeah, the other way round!" Daire had been horrified to find himself sighing and panting over that young fairy for a whole weekend.

"You didn't use it right—I told you!" Clove insisted. "Hey, you betting on the favorite?" He pointed at the track.

"Fiends' Fancy?" Daire pulled a face. "Nah."

"Mage's Girl?" Brackish asked, running his finger down the list of entrants.

"As if. No, my friends. I'm a firm believer in Lady Miracle." Daire jingled his bag of coins, making his friends' eyes bulge. He placed his wager with Aldon then rubbed his race slip between his palms and blew on it for luck.

"Be a miracle if that lady even places." Clove fancied himself an expert. On a lot of things. Funny, he was the opposite to Brackish, who tended to get the wrong end of the wand. Daire knew them well and they knew him. They'd been coming here for years. A decade or so. And he couldn't see things changing, imagine himself getting a partner. Daire squashed down the loneliness that had been bubbling up more and more in him. Things, his life—it was all…fine, wasn't it?

"Look—they're about to start!" another pixie shouted.

The bell clanged, the crowd roared and the jackalopes were released. A second later, and to a louder roar, the wind-hounds' gates were yanked up and the dogs streaked out in a series of mostly gray blurs. Daire whooped to see Lady Miracle in the lead, her jaws stretched out to take a chunk out of the tasty critter she was chasing. "Come on, my lady!" he yelled.

Lady Miracle lost. As did Elvish Has Left the Tavern in the next race and Pixies' Pride and Promise in the one after that.

"Troll shit! Speaking as a pixie, I can tell you you're not my pride and you broke any promise you might have made, you skinny mutt!" Daire yelled when the hounds, their tongues hanging from their panting mouths, were guided from the track.

Stuffing his useless betting slips into his mouth to chew and swallow, as custom dictated, Daire took stock of what he had left. It didn't take long. He wasn't the most prudent of gamblers.

"Time to call it a day then, loser?" Clove said, flicking Daire's empty pouch and making it swing.

"Nah. More like put everything on Hobgoblin's Hope in the five o'clock." Daire made for Oddsmaker Dalin. A longer walk, as that stall was farther away from the track, a result of the man's relative newness, but it was precisely Dalin's newbie status that made the effort worthwhile.

Whispering a transformation charm that he hoped would last long enough for his purposes, Daire was soon swinging a fat, shiny loud-ticking pocket watch by the fob of a short gold chain as he strolled.

"Why, hello there!" He pretended he'd only just now noticed Dalin and the little group around him and bet against himself which of them would be first to remark on what he held in his hand.

"Is this an actual *wasp*?" Dalin asked, his eyes enormous.

"A *watch*, yes." Daire wanted to roll his eyes. Dalin was too naïve to work in the profession he'd seemingly chosen. "From the human world, uh-huh." He counted the gasps this drew.

"You've been through the Veil?" whispered a pixie. Malpet, Daire thought his name was.

"Me? I go all the time!" Daire lied. "For my business, you know? Import-export. You'd be amazed at the demand for pixie semen — they use it in their medicine there!"

"No!" Dalin gasped.

No. Of course not. Daire nodded, pursing his lips. "And the things I bring back..." He left the bait dangling.

"Like...a wrist wasp?" Dalin asked, his voice hushed.

"A wrist*watch*?" Why was the oddsmaker so obsessed with timepieces — despite not knowing their correct name? Probably for the same reason most male pixies were, thinking it would make him look rich and cultured. Whatever. Daire didn't give a brownie's dangling nuts. "Sure! You seen the one Brackish's girlfriend's wearing?" Daire continued.

Brackish hadn't had a girlfriend since they were all in short breeches. Daire put that down to the general lumpiness of his forehead and had long suspected Brackish's real father was an orc. Orcs were green, and Brackish tended to take on a split-pea hue when he got emotional.

That notwithstanding, Malpet nodded. "Oh yes," he lied.

"Dainty little thing with no hands. The watch, I mean," Daire clarified, into the silence.

"I heard no hands and no numbers is the latest style," Malpet said.

"Yeah. You're in the know!" Daire favored him with a smile. "And they say they'll be making them with no straps next."

Daire waited for the murmurs that greeted this to settle, then reeled things in. "I go once a moon-cycle, so if anyone wants anything bringing back, just say. Oh, and pixie up the price in advance, obviously..."

He hadn't planned this scheme at all, but when life tossed a pack of gullible pixies into his path, it would be rude not to scoop up what they were so freely offering, wouldn't it?

"No problem, Klayburn," Daire assured the short bald pixie, pocketing his gold and writing down his request. "You'll get your sell-u-la-fone next week without fail."

Whatever a sell-u-la-fone was. Well, it didn't matter, when Daire wouldn't be able to get his pixie mitts on one, seeing that he'd never been anywhere near the Veil, let alone passed through it. He didn't even know where it was or what it looked like. "Right, then. If that's everyone and everything, I'll — "

"*Daire the pixie!*" The irate voice yelling close behind him cut him off. "Daire the cheating, lying, no-good pixie!"

Well, dung in a Sunday bucket. This couldn't be good...

Chapter Three

The mage dove through the empty window frame as if he were plunging into water, barely breaking his stride. They were two floors up, but Gage wasn't hopeful enough to think the mage would go plummeting to the ground and so put an end to their problems.

He was right. The mage's cloak floated up behind him, forming two large wings as black as his eyes. The wings beat back and forth, allowing him to hover in mid-air. He whirled around, laughing at Gage left behind in the corridor. "Like I said, it's as if I was never here," he sneered.

"You're an idiot," Gage replied, climbing into the window frame. "I mean, I knew you were stupid, but you're an actual *idiot*. Did you forget where you were? Griffin Guardians HQ. And what do griffins do? That's right..."

He didn't bother to complete his sentence but let his jump up into the air and his shift into his griffin form do it for him, showing this moron that griffins *flew*. The transformation was seamless. His smart gray uniform vanished. It would reappear later when needed, crisp and clean. Gage didn't understand how — he didn't think anyone did — but this bonus long-bestowed on the plane's Griffin Guardians was very useful for a shifter.

A griffin shifter. Gage, the tall, brawny soldier, was now an even more powerful creature, with the muscular tawny body, tail and back legs of a lion and the arrogant beaked head and wide, capable wings of an eagle. He took a second to relish the change to his other form, whipping his tail and flapping his wings the full extent of their span. Hooked eagle's talons, sharp and gleaming, comprised his animal's front feet, and Gage flexed them, feeling their strength and purpose.

Gage opened his beak, ululating an ear-splitting shriek. He was going to enjoy this! It had been too long since he'd pursued a quarry in his griffin form, the wind in his feathers and fur, the sky above him and the ground below him. The lion was considered the king of the beasts and the eagle the king of the birds, making a griffin formidable and giving the Griffin Guardians their well-deserved centuries-old reputations.

Modern, onerous directives and procedures, the increased number of links in the chain of command that made considerations and issued or denied permissions — it was all left behind when Gage took to the skies, his talons outstretched to seize his prey.

His shriek had served as a warning that he was hunting, a courtesy to the quarry he had within his sights, but the mage had been too stupid or too overconfident or too unskilled to flee quickly enough. Perhaps he'd been frozen in shock at Gage's transformation. Whatever the reason, Gage was almost disappointed to pierce through a black cloak-wing within seconds.

The mage screamed as Gage's claws tore through the wing, rending it in two like the cloth it was. He struggled, making the tear worsen, and pulled away as far as he could...to give himself room to spellcast. Of course. Gage had been expecting it.

Witchfire, flickering orange flames edged in blue, shot from the mage's fingers. "Ha!" the idiot exulted, shooting the flames at Gage.

The mage's remaining wing still fluttered, speeding the flames on their way, but even if the fire reached him, Gage doubted it would harm his chest feathers. Griffins grew stronger the longer they lived, and Gage was no spring eaglet, as the saying went. He opened his beak and breathed, snuffing the witchfire to nothing. The terror on the mage's face had Gage opening his beak wider, to let his laugh caw free.

Scowling, the mage twisted his hands together, almost like an old woman wringing them in distress. His lips worked, telling Gage he was casting, then he whipped his hands apart and pointed his fingers at Gage. Lightning leapt from the tips of the mage's nails, growing with each inch it traveled through the air, and each bolt aimed like an arrow at Gage.

"Thanks for the workout, idiot." Gage hoped his prisoner could catch what he was thinking. He whipped his tail from side to side, now curling it over his head, now curving in front of him from the left then the right, using it to knock each bolt out of the sky before it hit him.

It was a move that griffins—probably all tailed shifters—practiced from young gryphlinghood onward, deflecting small stones then bigger rocks. Repelling missiles with the tail like this was also a

Guardian training exercise, one Gage had mastered decades back and honed year on year.

His head tilted to one side, he regarded his prisoner, his meaning as clear as if he'd spoken — *that all you got?* The mage spluttered, his arms flailing, which gave Gage the idea to up the stakes a little. Issuing no warning, he opened his talons and let his prisoner drop a foot. "*Oops.*"

The mage's screams of fear blended with the whistle of the wind, and Gage enjoyed the sound for a moment before diving to re-capture a billowing piece of black fabric that was more cape than wing now. He tugged it hard, jerking the prisoner toward him and getting an up-close view of the fright on the mage's pale face. It made Gage open his beak, as if going to take a bite. He wouldn't, of course.

"Think you're so clever?" the mage gasped, recovering a little. "Deal with this, griffin!" *This* was his throwing a thunderbolt, a lightning strike that was strong enough to fry Gage and accompanied by a crash of thunder loud enough to disorientate him at best and deafen him at worst.

Gage smiled. Dedicated to improving his abilities, to widening his arsenal, he'd been one of the few Guardians to volunteer for assignments in the lava pits of Planzatillo, on the other side of the world, carrying out his duties in the midst of fire fairies and brontos demons. What he'd faced there meant he could ignore the eardrum-rupturing rolls of thunder and use his wings to swat away the lightning. It was almost like being back at the daily training he'd done in the lava realm.

Relishing the mage's shouts of frustration, he became aware of figures on the ground below, yelling commands or orders, but was too focused to let anything, any emotion, distract him.

When the angry, gibbering mage threw handfuls of ice-cold, stone-hard hail at him, clearly hoping to sting and even blind him, Gage felt a pang of pity for him. The missiles bounced off his feathers and fur. *So this is some jumped-up weather-mage, is it?* Well, whatever he was, Gage had had enough. Time to bring the prisoner in and make him face what he had coming.

He flicked his front leg up to shake the mage free of his talon as if he were of no more importance than a fly. The mage's screams in response to this held as much indignation as they did terror, but Gage ignored them. Half-turning in the air, Gage flung out his tail and used it as a rope, coiling it around the mage's middle, pinning his arms to his body to prevent any further spell casting—if the idiot had any more tricks in his bag—and pulling him closer.

Gage looked down. They hadn't flown far and were still over the Guardians' HQ. Over the grounds, in fact, with their pretty ornamental pond. It was more like a small lake, set out as a body of water for Guardians to relax around. As such, it was quite big...and deep enough for what he had in mind.

Gage plunged a little lower and unfurled his tail, letting his prisoner dangle headfirst over the pond, then drop down just a little bit more, making the mage's head break the surface of the water. Ooh, this was so un-Guardianlike, but so *good*. It vented a lot of his built-up frustration, both professional and personal.

He kept his captive under only for a few seconds, of course, before hauling him up, the mage spluttering and shaking wildly, spraying drops everywhere... which was when Gage dunked him again, for longer and to the shoulders this time. *"That's for Colm,"* he narrowcast, hoping the mage caught it.

"Stop! Help—I can't swim!" screeched the mage once Gage let him up this time.

Hm. Weather mage maybe, water mage definitely not. Gage nodded to tell his prisoner he'd heard him. He yanked the mage upward like a child's io-io toy, as if he were flying him away...only to dip him again for a third time. A longer, deeper final time, until the area around the pond was bustling with witnesses.

Gage shrugged. *"Sorry. I saved him but can't quite control my powers. Lots of magecraft in the air,"* he narrowcast, to whoever could pick up what he was putting out.

"Confess," he urged his prisoner. He doubted the mage could 'hear' but surely even this idiot must understand what Gage wanted from him.

"All right!" the mage squealed. "I did it. Tried to kill the Guardians who were after me for abusing my powers to steal money and goods! Now let me go?"

You asked for it... Gage jerked his tail free, letting the mage plummet into the pond with an enormous splash. He shifted back, his uniform reappearing and as spotless as ever, and would have helped fish the half-drowned prisoner out, if his name being boomed around the grounds hadn't stopped him.

"By the Goddess Ahndwa, you're in for it," muttered the second lieutenant Gage had booted out of the interrogation room earlier, wading into the water.

Gage thought so too, and knew so a half-hour later when, after keeping him cooling his wings in the anteroom outside, Commander Slate yelled at him to enter his office.

When Gage had first met his commander, he'd wondered if his name came from his hair, which had always been that dull gray from hatchlinghood on, its hues not changing much in all the years Gage had served under him. The color of his commander's face, on the other hand, varied more. Gage couldn't remember the color red, but knew faces flushed that color. Judging by the darker tone Slate's skin had acquired, his rage was rising high.

"Do you have any idea how many regs you ignored, flouted and broke?" the Guardian commander began, not giving Gage time to salute, or bothering with greetings at all.

"Not exactly, Sir," Gage admitted. Not with all the new directives about, but he started to tally up in his head the ones he was sure about.

"'Not exactly,'" Slate mimicked. "Well, a fuckload, is the correct answer!" He flicked at a sheaf of parchments on his desk.

"I did what it took to work the assignment. That prisoner should have been neutered, Commander," Gage replied.

"The neutralization paperwork was being processed!" Slate shouted. "I don't have a magic wand, to get these things done in a blink of fairy dust! And you do know that you shifted without permission? Oh wait. Of course you damn well do!"

"Sir, I refer you to my previous answer—I was getting the job done." Gage stood tall.

"And now the mage is claiming he was injured while in custody." Slate moved on to another piece of paper. "Oh no—attacked. *Mauled*! Mauled, it says here! Talon-slashed and tail-whipped."

Gage said nothing, just looked ahead.

Slate sighed. "Captain, I know your record and I admire it. I also know how you feel about the new directives that are—"

"Hamstringing us?" Gage threw in when Slate paused, clearly searching for a diplomatic word. "Or is that expression wrong? Would tying us in knots be better?"

"I can't say I totally disagree with that view," Slate admitted. "But with interspecies relationships a powder keg at the moment, you *know* what this makes us look like. It's been made clear to me that I have no choice but to stand you down from investigative duty." He shuffled the papers.

"To suspend me?" Gage couldn't believe it. "Sir, the corps is my whole life."

"Which isn't as good a thing as you seem to think. So maybe you can take time to reflect on that?" Slate stared hard at him.

"Commander, please." Gage didn't know what to say or do.

Slate exhaled. "Gage, I don't want to lose you. So what I can do is reassign you."

"To…" Gage didn't like the sound of it.

"Guard duty." Slate raised a hand to cut off Gage's protests that he was the best investigative griffin guardian they had, and that guard work was worse than grunt work—it was bullshit. "Shine brightly at this and you'll be back on regular duties as soon as it's over," he promised.

"Where?" Gage asked.

"Where? Let me see…" Slate turned over a page, but Gage had the feeling he knew and was enjoying this. "Where… Ah. At the World Magic Convention." His mouth twisting into a grin, he waited for Gage's exclamation to die down. "So if you think that's bullshit too, get ready to shovel."

"But it's in the Pixies Lands," Gage answered.

"Yeah, you're not a fan of the lesser beings, I recall." Slate nodded. "Pixies are tricky, goblins are grasping and all that? Then you're not gonna like this. In fact, you're really gonna hate it. Because, see, you're not just guarding one of the speakers, who I'm guessing is giving some nice hitting-all-the-buttons talk about respect and tolerance for all species, all of which deserve equal representation, blah-di-blah-blah. No, to show our commitment to interspecies equality, you're doing it with a *partner*."

"Sir?" Gage really didn't trust his commander's smile. "Colm is—"

"I know. I mean a new partner. A *local* partner."

"But the Convention's being held in the— You mean a *pixie*?" burst from him.

The look on Commander Slate's face was a full-blown smirk. "Yeah. I do. Well, you know what they say, Captain, that payback's a pixie bitch."

Chapter Four

"Daire the cheating, lying, swindling, double-dealing, no-good pixie!" the voice continued.

"You know, I don't tend to use my middle names much," Daire said, turning around...to see Oddsmaker Monops. *Ah. How much do I owe him?* And what other grievances did the oddsmaker have against him? The oddsmaker's one eye, glowing with the same rage that was in his voice, stared hard at the 'watch' Daire still held.

"Another 'watch', eh, Daire?" Monops swiveled his head to take in the group around Daire. "I only hope none of you bought it from him, because I guarantee you that 'watch' will be nothing but a turnip on a string come morning. Oh yes." He nodded at the exclaiming-out-loud group. "Look!" He pulled a small turnip on a string from his pocket.

Oh yeah. That. Now Daire remembered why he'd been trying to avoid him. *Oh gods, and that esmerald necklace for his wife...that was a handful of peas strung together.* He took a tiny step to one side. He didn't have a seeing-crystal, but he could see the way this was likely to go.

"How d'you even get in here, with your debts?" Monops demanded. "You owe me and half the oddsmen here, you cheating, lying —"

"No-good pixie. Yeah. We established that." Daire tried to calculate his chances and, not liking them, his exit route. "You should know, all of you…" Daire smiled as other racetrack pixies he owed money to swelled the group, like sea-sharks scenting blood. "That I'd be happy to pay my debts."

Of course he would. Having the amount of coin needed to discharge them would make him ecstatic.

Monops, probably suspecting a "But," advanced a little, swinging his turnip menacingly.

"Hey, careful!" Daire cautioned. "You'll put someone's eye out! Oh…is that what happened?" He indicated Monops' face with its black leather patch over one eye. "And did the same thing happen to your balls? Because you've only got one of those too, right?"

In the confusion his words created, he ran for it.

"I'll bust *your* balls when I catch you!" Monops yelled after him. "Turn your nutsac into a coin purse and keep all the money you owe me in it as an example to other pixies who think they can cheat me!"

"If I owe it to you, how can you put it in a purse?" Daire had to ask, over his shoulder, slowing a little to do so.

"When I get it, obviously, you cheating, lying, no-good — *Ow!*"

The crash Daire heard behind him was probably Monops banging into a kiosk and knocking it to the ground. With only having the one eye, Monops tended to bash into things and flatten them. Daire just didn't want one of those things to be him. He ran faster. Oh, why had he come to the tracks? He'd known Monops would be here. He just couldn't resist the thrill of a wager.

"Bet he's gonna get you this time," Brackish called out as Daire raced by.

"Oh yeah?" Daire skidded to a halt. "How much and what odds?" See? He was doing it again! Yelling, "A twenty says he doesn't get me—you in?" over his shoulder, he sprinted away, out of the raceway.

"You won't run far when I break your legs!" Monops shouted behind him.

"Oh, I see you're a bit of a philosopher," Daire called back in reply.

"You slow down and take what's coming to you!" yelled another voice, probably someone else he owed money to, and who was maybe too old or out of shape for pursuit.

Daire declined. In fact, he sped up. He'd soon shake them off, especially if he took a shortcut around the market square—

"*There* he is! Right *there*, look!" cried a voice.

What the seven hells? Daire stared aghast at the remnants of his audience from earlier, who were telling their sorry stories to a patrol pixie. Half a dozen of them were pointing at him and tugging on the patrol pixie's arm.

"Daire!" yelled Patrol Officer Navin, picking up a stone and throwing it after him.

"Ow!" Daire yelled. Navin's aim was improving. *Must be all the practice.* He dashed through the market, darting along the aisles and zigzagging around the stalls. What in the name of the Great God Lollygag was he going to do now? Catching sight of Glannet, the apothecpixie, and his wares, gave Daire an idea.

"Glannet!" he called. "I need a changeling charm! Quick!"

"Male or female change?" Glannet called back.

"Female?" Daire hadn't thought that far ahead.

"Blonde or brunette?" Glannet shouted.

"I don't care — *blonde*. Blonde!" Daire yelled.

"Basic charm or enhanced?" Glannet bellowed.

"I don't know!" Daire yelped, reaching the wooden barrow Glannet sold his goods from. "Basic?" It had to be cheaper. "Quick!" He cast an anguished look over his shoulder at the bustle coming from the market entrance behind him.

"Enhanced is better. Customer is always right though." Glannet sighed. "Size? Fairy or troll?" He held out the different bottles. "Troll is better value."

"*Fairy!*" Daire fumbled for his emergency coin.

"Flavored or plain? Flavored is — *Rude!*" Glannet exclaimed when Daire grabbed the smaller bottle and shoved his last coin into Glannet's hand in exchange.

Daire unstoppered the container and guzzled the contents. "*Bleerggh!*" he squealed, nearly throwing up.

"Told ya flavored was better." Glannet dropped the coin into the leather pouch strapped around his middle.

Daire didn't stop to debate the point. He couldn't, not when a bang sounded inside his head, something shook him hard enough that his teeth rattled and the looking-glass at the end of the clothing stall opposite no longer reflected an average-sized, chestnut-haired male pixie but a tall, slim blonde female one.

And rather a looker. He still looked the same to himself if he looked himself up and down, but the sexy blonde was what other people would see.

"Nice one," he muttered.

"He went this way!" someone shouted, and a section of the crowd rushed along the aisle where Daire stood…and hurried right past him.

"He's along there!" Daire called in a high-pitched voice, pointing over his shoulder, smiling as his pursuers fell for it. He took a couple of mincing steps back the way he'd come when *bang!* and *rattle!* and he was himself again, the charm over.

"Oh, what?" he yelled. "That didn't even last a minute!"

"Told you to take the enhanced, and the bigger bottle." Glannet shrugged.

"That's him there!" screeched a woman, and the section of the crowd who'd run past him raced back, colliding with those in the rear, who'd just caught up.

"Here, this coin's chokolat!" Glannet thundered behind him.

"Oh, dung on a mushroom!" Daire shoved through the still remaining gap in the middle of the two clumps of people after him and hurtled for the exit.

There was a short row of stores on the edge of the market and Daire nipped into the first, thinking to shimmy out through the emergency exit that must be at the back, when the store's display window caught his eye.

He'd never shopped here, and often scoffed at the clothes that In The Closet sold, but now he was glad the store carried stupidly big hats and garish all-enveloping cloaks. He hopped into the window and grabbed a cartwheel-sized red hat from the dummy to his right and a purple and red cloak the size of a double bedsheet from the one on his left.

Feeling he needed more, he snatched up a necklace, its links as big as dinner plates, and dropped it over his head, then plucked a hand fan from a rack. When splayed out, it was the width of a dressing screen. *Perfect.* All he had to do was stand still and let his pursuers run past. He struck a pose and breathed as shallowly as he could.

"I'm sorry, sir. I'll do it right away, sir." promised the short, skinny pixie backing from the store into the window area, bowing as he did so. "I simply didn't have time to change the window display earlier, sir." He spun around and grabbed the dummy nearest to him, yanking at its buttons.

"Perhaps if you weren't too mean to hire enough help, all the jobs that need doing would get done, *sir!*" he muttered, pulling the dress off. "Or, perhaps if you had one iota of taste, you could do this job yourself, *sir!*" He grabbed at the next dummy, which was Daire—and screamed.

"It's warm and breathing—I said they'd come back to life!" he whimpered, sliding to the floor.

"Rudolfo?" Daire thought he recognized the pixie from the Cockpit on the city limits. Unless his memory played him false, they'd hooked up.

"It knows my name!" Rudolfo was now curled into a ball, rocking back and forth.

"What's going on here?" The owner of In The Closet was made of sterner stuff, or perhaps more used to miscreants hiding in his shop window, and took in the situation at a glance. "Shoo!" he ordered, brandishing a broom. "Shoo, I say! Begone!"

Daire shooed and was gone, shedding oversized accessories and the violently colored cloak as he did so. "Yes, there he is," he said before any of the posse after him could, when he was once again pounding the pavement.

Gods, he was tired. And, oh no, approaching the tavern, the Pixie's Neck, where he'd run up a big tab. And another. And another. Well, if the landlord Adam the Dwarf was dumb enough to believe Daire was triplets…

Still, the sight of the door trolls slapping their heavy clubs into the palms of their free hands had Daire reversing direction, which took him toward the big white building at the top of the town. Oh, of course! He'd never had much use for such a place before, and didn't really believe, but a hurried glimpse at the size of the crowd after him and feeling the heat of their anger had him converted. He burst through the big doors.

"Sanctuary!" he gasped, falling to his knees. "I seek…" *Wait a minute.* This building looked too official, and that big table and chair up there on that raised platform… "Sanctuary?" He got up slowly. "This…? The church…?"

"Is next door," the uniformed official said.

"So this is…?" Daire swallowed.

"The court." Another clerk allowed the crowd of arguing, accusing, shouting plaintiffs in, then slammed the door and barred it. "Is in session!" he announced. "And Daire the pixie, while you are often summoned, this is the first time you've appeared."

"But—" Daire tried. Gods, he detested any form of authority and this most of all.

But nothing. Calling out, "All breaks canceled—this is going to be a long one," the clerk dragged him to the dock with the other accuseds.

"Arlen, Tranell." Daire nodded at the ones nearest — he knew most of them.

"Daire. Seen who it is?" Tranell pointed at the judge. "Hard as Nails Naylor. And she's mad as hells."

The lady pixie judge got madder as she read Daire's charges. "Daire the pixie, do you know how much trouble you're in?" she inquired.

"No, but if you hum it, I'll try to pick it up?" Daire pulled his pfeife free. "Ready when you are. One-two-three — *Ow*." He glared at the clerk who'd hit him around the head. These officials must have to have their sense of humor removed when they took up their post.

"I don't know if I should do this alphabetically or in categories or in chronological order!" Judge Naylor snarked, tapping a long bloodred-painted fingernail on his chargesheet. She looked over at Daire's accusers. "Shall we draw lots for it? Or is anyone in a hurry and needs to go first?"

Adam the Dwarf raised a hand. Clicks of his stumpy fingers had his security trolls bending down for him to step onto their hands, a foot on each palm, for them to raise him high enough for his hand to be seen.

"Very well." The judge nodded. "Let's start with unpaid tavern bills."

Adam the Dwarf was still hoisted high enough for the gesture he made in Daire's direction, him drawing a finger across his throat, to be seen.

"And move on to selling pixie powder to gullible tourists — powder that was dried troll dung!" The judge indicated a small group of ill-looking people. "And what's this about a cure for acne? What was it made from? Some words are hard to read, as if the court scribe were shaking or weakened —"

The clerk approached to whisper in her ear. Her eyes widened and her mouth dropped open. "Harvested at full moon?" She stared at Daire's crotch. "Well, I have no doubt he has plenty of the fluid in question, but I sincerely doubt he's a virgin, so that's false claims, right there. And add today's thefts from tourists…"

Her scowl matched the one in her portrait that hung on the wall above her chair. "Because of pixies like you, the wider plane thinks we're all shiftless, feckless petty crooks."

Daire shrugged. It seemed a fair assessment to him.

"You don't care that you're single-handedly giving pixies a bad name? Maybe you will when I have you make reparations for the damages you've caused us as a race." Judge Naylor motioned to the clerk to smack Daire again.

Daire rubbed his head where the clerk slapped it. "So, litter duty, is it?" He'd done it before. No biggie. And the things that pixies threw away… He recalled all those drafts of the ode that Waelo had written to Drina…that he hadn't wanted his wife Perneilope to see. Daire had done well out of Waelo's infatuation. Well, so had Drina. And Perneilope, in the divorce.

"Not…quite." The judge's smile held malice. "I'm going to have you work toward restoring our people's reputation…by sentencing you to work as the local liaison at the World Magic Convention being held here in the capital."

Daire shrugged again, harder. He'd soon duck out of things. Use a few charms…

"Oh, I forgot to add…" The judge's smile dripped poison. "That this will be after being stripped of whatever magic you've managed to—I'm sure—

illegally acquire. Clerk? If you'd be so kind to take the sentenced to the removing room?"

"What? *No!*" Daire wailed.

Fiends and fairies—he might actually have to work now, and at some stupid convention with some snobby dragon or stuck-up wyvern.

Could life get any crappier?

Chapter Five

Daire, his head still spinning, his stomach still roiling and his skin still stinging from his encounter with the Court-appointed shaman, scowled at the clerk who was hurrying the sentenceds outside.

"Oh, what?" he demanded. "You're kidding me! The community service starts right *now*? Come on! I'll start first thing tomorrow. Bright and early. Sunrise. Before sunrise. Up with the larks. Before the larks. You can trust me!"

The clerk snorted and shoved him into the official Court cart that stood waiting in the yard, its four paards harnessed and blinkered, but managing to look tough and mean.

"Look, there's no need for me to go in this rattletrap, you know. Let's spare the horses, and I'll make my own way to my community service on my own two pixie feet," Daire told the patrol officer who was taking over their escort from the clerk.

The patrol officer snorted too. *They must teach it during training.* "I look green to you?" he scorned, tapping the driver on the shoulder to tell him they were ready to go.

Daire tilted his head. "Hm, face more like a potato than a cabbage, if you want my opinion," he replied.

"I don't. So shut up. You'll live longer," the officer advised.

Daire shut up...for at least five minutes. "Hey, let me out here and I'll walk the rest of the way," he said next, when the convention center came into sight. "I don't want anyone to see me hanging out with a bunch of sentenceds and a patrollee. No offense."

With a hearty laugh, the officer took him from the cart right to the main door. "Look, count yerself lucky. This 'un's going to the stocks," he said, jerking his thumb over his shoulder at another sentenced.

"Yeah, bye, Clove," Daire called. He waved. *Anyway, now to duck out of this crap.* This world convention bullshit didn't start until tomorrow and there weren't many people about yet. Even so, he huddled against the wall to one side of the doors and checked no one was looking before he peeled the sticky plaster from the roof of his mouth.

And was he glad to get rid of it—the chish pad, made of a paste designed to protect the wearer against having his powers stripped from him, tasted like sewers smelled...and how his breath no doubt smelled. It had cost a pretty penny too. Still, as long as it worked, he'd endure.

"Thanks, Clove," Daire muttered to the seller, currently being trundled away, and got to thinking, fast. Okay, yep, he'd send a shadowform into the convention place, to make it look like he was there. He could just about manage that with the stuff he had on him that hadn't been found. Fine, he'd have to wear a disguise as he went about his business in town for a couple of days, but no biggie. So, now to cast the —

Nothing. *Damn.* He tried harder, jumping up and down and shaking out his hands at the cramps in his fingers and toes that his attempts caused. The itch down his spine had him scraping his back down the wall to scratch it. Third time lucky? "*Yearrgh!*" This try had him clapping his hands around his head when his brain tingled. Still nothing. *Shit!* That tricksy pixie Clove had conned him!

Daire cursed the swindling pixie for at least five minutes. "The stocks're too good for you, you cheating bastard!" he finished at last. He took a look down the street. He could just not turn up for this crap, but non-compliance with community service spelled instant jail time. Ogres' assholes! He hated how authority was all up in everyone's business, not letting a pixie make a dishonest living!

He had no choice but to head for the huge building. It was even bigger than the Court, and he didn't like big buildings. They weren't natural to pixies. "Ooh, let's build a convention center in the Pixies Lands. Every species this side of the Veil will want to come to our capital to hold events here," he mimicked.

The pixies had competed with the fairies for the project. The Frolic Lands should have won the right to build it, for all Daire gave a crap. The pixie kingdom had been taxed heavily to pay for the construction and fitting out, too. Well, those of its citizens who paid tax...

He stamped his heel down on the ground to relieve his feelings and, when that didn't work, brought his foot back and kicked at a large stone lying on the path. He must have been angrier than he thought because he kicked harder than he'd intended. The stone flew through the air and —

"*Hey!*"

— hit a mountain. Well, a mountain of a person. A tall, broad and uniformed mountain of a non-pixie person. Who turned and glared down his haughty nose at Daire. Daire shivered.

"You there!" The deep voice sent a tingle down Daire's spine to take the place of the itch.

Daire had never gone for authority before — he usually fled from it, in fact — but thought he might just make an exception for Blondie here, mainly as he couldn't take his eyes from him. That tall body. That chiseled face. That firm ass. That —

"Did you just kick a fucking stone at me?"

— fury at having been assaulted.

"Who, sir? Me, sir? No. It wasn't me, sir. I was in the tavern, sir. A dozen pixies'll swear to that, sir." His answer came automatically, honed over the years, and he stood his ground as the mountain marched toward him.

"Oh. *I* see." Blondie tilted his head back more to look down his aquiline nose. He had thick eyelashes, the same color as his hair, and his full lips were twisted as his narrowed blue-eyed gaze raked Daire up and down. *Arrogant and prejudiced.* Typical of Daire's luck. He should know by now that a uniform was a uniform, no matter how fucking sexy its wearer.

The stranger tossed the stone that he must have caught — Daire admired his reflexes — into the air and palmed it again. "Well, you're lucky I'm in too much of a hurry to deal with you, pixie."

"Thanking ye kindly, sir." Daire swept off his floppy hat and bowed low. He made a performance of standing upright again, his hand on his lower back and a pained grimace on his face, relishing the matching scowl the newcomer made on clearly catching a whiff of Daire's chish breath.

"Well?" the stranger demanded after a slight pause.

"Well what?" Daire was perplexed.

"Clear off!" the stranger ordered. "You have no reason to be loitering here. Especially with an offensive weapon—your breath." He fanned the air between them, then, giving Daire a final stern look that had Daire hardening in his pants, Soldier-Boy swept away...inside the center. *He must be working here too.*

A wicked thought curved Daire's lips. Oh, he was going to enjoy this. He threw a sprig of spearedmint into his mouth to chew, to take care of his breath. Then, ambling inside, he strolled after the guy who must have felt his presence, because he whipped around. The confusion on his face made Daire happy. Maybe no one had ever disobeyed the stranger before. Well, he'd find out how Daire reacted to orders.

"Spare a coin, kind sir?" Daire said, before Blondie could speak. He plucked his pfeife from its loop on his belt. "I'll give you a tune, so I will." He lifted the instrument to his lips and blew. Badly. Catching sight of a team of caterers bustling about made him add, "Could ye spare a crust, too, sir?"

The stranger—Daire got a winged-beast feel from him and thought *griffin*—eyed him. "There's a ward on the door, so only authorized personnel can enter. So..."

He paused, studying Daire, who wondered what kind of picture he presented in his far-from-clean pants, blouson shirt and half-cloak, his stuffed-full knapsack on his shoulder, especially compared to this regulation-perfect creature in this formal setting.

The possibly-a-griffin pointed at Daire's pfeife. "Are you…entertainment?"

Daire couldn't resist that. "I'd keep *you* amused with my instrument," he replied, his wink enormous. Should he add a kiss to his words?

"Oh, gods above. You're a good-time pixie?" The blond took a step back. "A, what do they call it now…a sex worker?"

"Me? Nah. I don't like to work at anything, me," Daire replied. He spied a caterer carrying a tray of little dishes and, when the pixie came near enough, Daire helped himself to a small nut-brot roll and slice of sauteed kow tongue, with the caterer being none the wiser.

"Oh, of course." The griffin curled a lip.

"Of course what? And what's that condescending roll of the lip for?" Daire demanded, imitating it. Well, a version of it, all sour mouth and pained expression.

"Just that I hadn't understood how accurate the stereotypes are. Pixies." The blond waved at Daire. "Being lazy, work-shy, wanting something for nothing. Total freeloaders."

"Is that right?" Daire finished his snack and stepped nearer, until he was toe to toe with the stranger. "And I know your sort too." He poked him in the chest. The strong, firm chest. "Griffins…trying to rule and regulate everything, sticking your beak into every last nook and cranny. A busybody, with no life outside the job. I bet you haven't had a date this side of the last equinox, and as for the last time you got laid—ha! Get signed written permission in triplicate first, did you? Bet *that* wasn't worth the parchment."

He poked the griffin again, even though it hurt his finger. "Or the ink."

He went to tap the stranger's chest again on the last word, to make his point, but found his hand seized in a much larger, stronger one before he could make contact again. The griffin knocked his hand away, the force pushing Daire with it, and it got him mad. Mad enough to form his hand into a fist, leap up and land a blow on that handsome, arrogant, handsome, superior face, the surprising force of his punch making the griffin stagger backward.

"Why, you little—" Recovering in an instant, the griffin shoved Daire in the chest in retaliation, his strength knocking Daire onto his ass.

"Get down here and say that!" Daire ordered him.

"My pleasure." The stranger bent and hauled Daire to his feet and into the air with one hand, pulling back the other to strike him again, just as Daire drew back a leg to kick him.

"Is…is there a problem here?" asked a hesitant voice.

The arrival of a uniformed pixie, the badge around his neck denoting that he was a convention center employee, had them both freezing, like they were performing some artistic living picture display on a stage, then replying "No," at the same time.

"Put. Me. Down," Daire ordered.

"Of course." The griffin dropped Daire. On his ass. Again. "Oh. Want me to help you up?" He lifted his foot, his meaning clear.

"Want me to help you *mop* up?" Daire stood and pointed at the trickle of blood oozing from the griffin's nose.

"I…see you've met," the employee said.

"*Met*?" Daire asked. He had a bad feeling about this. "Met who?"

"Your, erm, well, partner." The organizer gave a little laugh, waving a weak finger from Daire to his opponent and back again.

"*What*?" Daire growled.

" *— the five hells*?" the griffin finished for him, growling louder.

"Captain Gage of the Griffin Guardians, and Daire the pixie, local liaison, comprising the escort-guard for VIP guest number one," the organizer blurted, all in one breath. He didn't look any happier about things than they did. His smile was strained as he attempted to hand over two paper files.

Staring hard at each other, neither Daire nor Gage took them.

"I'll just leave all this here, shall I?" the employee whispered, and had deposited his paperwork on a table and slid away before he'd finished speaking.

"*Partner*?" Daire burst out at the same time as Gage roared "*Team*?"

Neither blinked, glaring daggers at the other.

Eventually, Daire sighed. "Call it even?" he asked, holding out a hand. As the griffin frowned, maybe trying to work out Daire's meaning, that perhaps he intended to request a cease-fire, Daire clenched his hand into a fist and punched him again. In the balls. Making him double over and groan. "Well, it is now," Daire judged, adding up how many hits each had gotten in.

The griffin—*Cage? What kind of a name is that?*—straightened up, his eyes watering. "Truce?" he asked, his voice a little higher than it had been. He coughed.

"Sure." Daire could afford to be magnanimous now he'd paid his stupidly tall, ridiculously broad-shouldered and unnecessarily firm-assed opponent back. With interest. He smiled and offered the griffin his handkerchief to clean his annoyingly handsome face.

The griffin took it and dabbed up the blood. "Thanks. Pear, is it, your name?"

"*Daire*. You're Rage, right? And corporal, didn't that admin pixie say?"

"*Gage. Captain* Gage." The shrewd gleam in the griffin's sky-blue eyes suggested he knew Daire was pulling his tail. "For a being so small, you've got a good right hook," he commented.

"That's nothing. Wanna see my left swipe?" Daire asked.

"Left...*swipe*?" Gage's forehead creased, as if he were trying to recall a move with that name.

"Sure!" Daire was tracking the approach of a caterer, who was pushing a trolley that held a number of trays. One bore gleaming crystal goblets of ruby-red vin, and this was the tray Daire liberated in a clean swipe, this employee also continuing on his way oblivious. Daire went to offer his spoils to Gage, but the look on the griffin's face, one sour enough to spoil the vin, stopped him.

Chapter Six

"Oh, *of course*," Daire sneered, trying to look down his nose, as difficult as that was because it was turned up.

What? That little good-for-nothing was mimicking him! Gage swelled with the same sensation of injury he'd felt when the pixie had punched him in the face. *Had gotten in that lucky blow,* he self-corrected, glaring down at the creature who stood at least a foot shorter than him.

Not that Gage had even felt the strike land. It was his pride that was wounded, but not in the sense of him feeling personally affronted at the half-pint managing to lay a hand on him. The shame flickering through Gage was at having struck back at a lesser being. Or lower creature or whatever they had to be called these days.

It was ingrained in the more noble higher beings, or winged ones or whatever the dawn and dusk Gage was known as now, that they were more powerful than the earthern races — *isn't that the latest approved term?* — and shouldn't harm them in any way. Creatures with more natural advantages shouldn't exploit those below them.

But this one, standing there imitating what Gage had said to him earlier, seemed determined to get under Gage's feathers and fur. *Daire.* Gage wanted to snort fire at the name. Why did they all have to have such silly ones? They were all called Klang and Krashe and Flaile-About and things like that. Daire set down the tray he'd just *stolen* on the small table in a nearby alcove where the other pixie had left their instruction packs.

"I understand. That stick stops you drinking, right?" he asked.

"Stick?" Gage asked.

"Yeah, that stick up your ass!" Daire sniped. "That stick up your ass that's got its own stick up its ass!" He raised a goblet to Gage, as if saluting his own wit, and drank its contents in one long swallow, his head thrown back, his red-brown waves of hair sweeping and flowing.

"Or maybe it's that you don't trust yourself around alcohol," the pixie continued, sympathy in his lilting voice. He took up another goblet in a long-fingered hand. "Lightweight, are you?" Daire knocked this drink back too, his lively eyes fixed on Gage over the rim of the cup.

Oh, that was too much. This lesser being might be attractive, in a shiny-green-eyed, full-red-lipped *pixie* kind of way—but he was an irritating, provocative, twinkling, beguiling— "Lightweight, me?" Gage roared.

"Not your actual...tonnage." Daire lowered his voice, indicating Gage's body. "Sure, you could stand to lose a pound or two, but, well. My understanding is you wing-dings — sorry, wingeth-beasts, right? Have to keep up with the language of the time — don't walk or run all that much, do you?

"Wh — ?" Gage tried to interrupt.

"So the weight just piles on?" Daire trailed his gaze down Gage's body to land it on his stomach. He pulled a rueful face

"I-I'm in perfect physical shape, I'll have you know!" Gage spluttered. "You only have to look at me to see!" He stood tall, shoulders back and chest out as if on parade. Why was he puffing himself up for this pixie, a con-artist who was used to reading his audience and seeing which feathers to pull? Did he want this pixie to look at him?

"And hey, not being able to hold your drink is nothing to be ashamed of." A smirk on his uptilted lips, Daire reached for a third cup.

"*What*? I can outdrink you any day of the week and twice on high days and holidays, pipsqueak!" Gage protested, stung. To prove it, he snatched up a glass in each hand and tipped the contents of one then the other down his throat, fighting not to gasp at the burn. Mermaids' tails, the vin was strong.

Daire scoffed. "That the best you can do, beaky?" He hefted two goblets in each hand and drank all four, two at a time. "That's how pixies drink."

"That's how trolls drink, half-pint," Gage corrected, fighting the slight swimming in his head. He hadn't realized the vin was fortified. "But that's typical, because pixies are parasites. Oh, excuse me, 'borrowers'. How's that saying go? To make one pixie, take the charm of the fairies — "

"Thank you kindly." Daire drank to that.

"The earth magic of the elves..." Gage stared as Daire took a sip at that too. "Although it's weaker and you have to use lotions and potions to work any enchantment." That earned another drink. "The cunning of goblins, and the law and order of the winged beings." He hurried on before Daire could drink more. "Except it's all for nothing, because you have the manners of giants, the brains of orcs and the breath of trolls!"

This Gage thought worthy of drinking to and saluted the pixie with a glass on the strength of it. He drained it. "Yeah, all mixed into one — "

"Cocktail?" Daire offered, helping himself to two ornate goblets the size of fishbowls as a waiter carried them past.

"Huh?" he asked when the one he lifted to his mouth didn't release any liquid. He shook it. It sloshed but didn't slop over the rim of the cup.

Gage sighed. "You don't have any learning, do you? Those are twain cups. You can't drink from your own." When Daire didn't get it, he sighed louder. "You drink from the other?"

Daire tried, taking up the other cup with the same result.

"Oh, for crying at the gates of dawn. Like this." Exasperated, Gage sank into a sit on the small table. He took one of the goblets from Daire, wound his arm around Daire's and held the cup to his mouth. "Now drink."

Daire did, his throat working as he swallowed. He smacked his lips, which were now rosier than they had been. His pale face was a little pinker too. It made his eyes look a more vivid green. "By the suns above, that's good! It must be vintage. Here, try it."

He crooked his arm over Gage's, then went to lower it. "Oh, sorry. Forgot about your weakness, and this is a little strong. It'd have you on your *knees*."

A shiver went down Gage's spine at that, and he fought it along with the image Daire's words evoked — Gage on his knees before this infuriating…pretty pixie. He shot out a hand to tilt Daire's wrist and hold it steady — he wouldn't put it past the tricksy pixie to slop vin down him — and bent his head to drink. He didn't gasp this time either, but he did splutter. So he took another swallow to soothe his throat…and choked.

"Yeah, I should have said *very* strong, not *quite* strong. My bad." But no sorrow or apology peeped from the pixie's eyes to accompany his words. Instead, merriment danced in their flecks, flecks Gage was close enough to see. How many shades of green made up Daire's eyes? They were a range of hues from a deep forest to a glittering esmerald. That he even noticed confused him, so he drank the rest of the vin…because it was there, he supposed.

"Well, that's halfway," Daire commented, placing both cups down.

"Halfway?"

"That the stick's dislodged." Daire grinned, looking like the poster boy for pixies. "Maybe you're not a completely joyless, stuck-up by-the-book wing-ding after all."

"Wait." It only now struck Gage that Daire had chestnut hair and green eyes. Gage could see them. But griffins didn't see in color, not once they left gryphlinghood. As mature adults, they saw in black and white and shades of gray. So why — ? He forced his brain to stop swimming and work.

Was it a Pixies Lands thing? Things had all looked normal as he'd made his way here, but perhaps the magic or whatever it was here worked slowly? He cast a look around. No, the hall he was in looked as he'd expect it to. Oh, this pixie must be a strong magic user, and remnants of the last charms or enchantments he'd used were clinging to him! Interesting. No, more than that. Fascinating. Beguiling. He smiled.

"I know—I hear it too! It's coming from there!" Daire jerked his head to the left.

"Hear..." Gage strained to hear above the sounds of the center's staff preparing the space for the start this time tomorrow. But yes, there was a rattling, or a shaking, and the noise of something or things small and wooden being thrown. Voices rose too. "What—?"

But the pixie was gone.

"It's a gaming room!" Daire stood in a narrow doorway, peeping in, his voice as squeaky-high in his excitement that shone from him.

"A casino?" Gage asked.

"Cass-een-oh." Daire tried the word out, sticking his head and shoulders in.

"They're quite popular in big venues like this and— Wait a minute! We can't go in there!" Gage started, breaking off when Daire rushed back. "Exactly. We're not here for that. We don't start until tomorrow, but we should be doing reconnaissance, making sure we know the terrain, checking the locations of all ingresses and egresses and assessing that—"

"We can access all areas!" Daire pulled his pass from his information pack and kissed it. "Oh, you thing of beauty!" He bounded off.

"Daire!" Gage shouted, almost falling when he went to go after him—he'd forgotten he was sitting down.

"We need to check the rooms, so we can start there, right?" Daire called, already halfway into the casino.

He had a point, Gage supposed, picking up their folders and following, his steps a little tottery. He caught up with Daire just inside, where he was staring from table to table, from game to game, his face an agony of indecision.

"The room looks fine. Now come away." Gage pointed at the door.

"What?" A look of disappointment washed over Daire. "Oh, beaky. And I thought we'd dislodged it. The—"

"I do not have a stick up my ass!" Gage yelled, grimacing when the gamers and players, and the casino staff, all turned to stare. "I do not..." he started to whisper, but Daire had gone.

"Gage, look, Dirty Pig!" His face one big beam, Daire beckoned Gage over to a table. He patted at his pockets and his face fell. "Lend me a coin until we get paid? Or actually, until I win it back? And I'll give you half my winnings, just as you would me, right? Oh, unless we get a couple of throws free, being staff?" He shot a glass-green wink at the croupier.

Gage gaped. There was so much wrong with what Daire had just said and done. Behaving like that toward that croupier pixie? "I most certainly will not lend you any coin to lose at this...this game of jeopardy!" he spluttered.

"It's not Jeopardy—it's Dirty Pig!" Daire looked as though Gage had insulted his mother.

"Yes, a game where players roll a single die as many times as they like to see who gets the highest score... and where you lose if you roll a one," Gage scoffed.

"But I'm good at it!" Daire protested.

"Until you jeopardize what you have by trying for more." Gage could imagine. "There's no discipline in that."

"Discipline?" Daire looked like he'd never heard the word before. "Like strategy?"

"No." Gage looked around. "Like…science."

Before Daire could ask what he meant, Gage was at the primero table. "Deal me in," he demanded, taking a seat. He'd show that pixie. There were systems to things. Order. Method.

"A card game? That's…" Daire, when he reached the table, might have been intending to make a scornful remark, but his mouth dropped open when Gage won that hand. "That's…" he tried again when Gage won the second.

It was easy for Gage to see the likelihood of which cards were in play, along with who was bluffing, and, within minutes, who he could induce to raise or to fold. He doubted any of the others had played against a griffin shifter, used to reading people and seeing their tics, before.

When he won the third and final hand of the round and the card-master pushed the coins toward him, Daire whooped, leaning over to scoop half into his money bag. With an, "Oh, you fantastic flying beast!" he grabbed Gage's face in both hands and smacked his lips to Gage's in a kiss.

It might have been intended as a happy spontaneous thank-you, but at the meeting of their lips, something shot through Gage. Dazed, he tried to categorize it, but could only feel the raw joy of being *alive* and *here* and *now*. He gasped.

"Did you — ?" Daire pulled away enough to ask but didn't complete his thought. He licked his lips instead and the sight of his tongue moving over his flesh had Gage mesmerized. A crease between Daire's brows and his glittering green eyes on Gage's, he angled his face to slowly rub the tip of his turned-up nose against Gage's more aquiline one. "Pixie kiss," he muttered.

Gage hadn't realized he had nerve endings in the tip of his nose, but he must have, because they woke up, thrumming, at the gentle touch and all he could do was gasp again. And act in kind.

"Griffin kiss," he whispered, his lips against Daire's. The touch was soft, a gentle testing or perhaps an exploration, until Daire slanted his head to one side and slid his tongue across Gage's bottom lip.

Gage knew without knowing how he knew that Daire wanted him to open his mouth for a deeper kiss. He obeyed, his heart jolting at the first touch of the pixie's tongue against his, then groaned as Daire ground his mouth against his, caressing the inside of Gage's mouth with slow intent.

When Daire pulled free, it was to glide his lips down to the pulse beating fast in the side of Gage's neck, to make it speed more, and make Gage moan.

"What...?" Gage tried to say. *Is happening? Is this? Are you doing? Are we doing?* None of them came out, but maybe Daire understood, because he grinned that wicked grin.

"Well, we've had a drink and a date, so there's only one thing left, wouldn't you say?"

"And that's—?" Gage managed to ask.

"Why, a fuck." Daire's grin was loaded with pure pixie promise.

Chapter Seven

"Wait!" Gage tore his mouth free of Daire's. "We can't—"

Daire groaned. "Don't go all griffin shifter on me now, soldier."

Griffin? Oh right. He was. One whose back was currently pressed against the wall, despite him having no memory of having staggered across the gaming room, propelled there by the sexy pixie grinding on him. "Room," he gasped. "No—" He grabbed Daire when he went to back away. "We room. Us room. Not here."

"Oh. Yeah." The chuckle Daire gave, despite sounding strained, was dirty. "Come on."

Only two problems, Gage thought, or tried to think. Could they make it to the room they'd been allotted? And where the hells was it? Daire stopped groping Gage's ass long enough to scoop up their information files from the floor just inside the casino room where he'd dropped them earlier, and Gage stopped fondling

Daire's ass for the second it took to snatch up his pack where he'd left it in the main entrance hall.

He'd never walked up a flight of stairs backward and kissing before but supposed he did now, because the next thing he knew, he and Daire were in a narrow corridor then inside a small bedroom, and need was sizzling every vein in his body. He grabbed Daire, pressing that sexy body hard to his.

"Well, hello," Daire commented, cupping Gage's bulge. "That's never an official part of Guardians dress. Can't be regulation size. And the way your ass looks in these pants? I need to see if it's the cut of the fabric, or if it's really that good."

Gage tried to capture Daire again, wanting to sink his tongue deep into the pixie's mouth and yank that lithe body against his. No, get Daire flat on his back, spreading his legs, purring—pixies purred, didn't they?—and moaning for him. Offering himself up to him. But all he could do was stand there and take it as Daire explored him. *Enjoyed* him.

Daire's slim fingers opened Gage's tunic and he used one hand to caress his chest. The other was still squeezing Gage's ass cheek. Daire's thumb came to rest over Gage's nipple, and he rubbed, exclaiming in satisfaction when it hardened and Gage shivered. "Sensitive!" Daire gloated and replaced his fingers with his mouth.

Heat flared through Gage at the first touch and threatened to burn him up as Daire sucked and nipped, first one nub then the other, leaving them stiff, aching peaks. Gage panted for air, overwhelmed.

"Hey." Daire must have seen that Gage was about ready to come in his pants. With a crooked smile, he stretched up to nuzzle into Gage's neck. Nuzzle then suck, hard enough to leave a mark. He'd said he didn't like working, but he was busy now, easing Gage's tunic from him, and stroking every inch of flesh he uncovered.

Gage had always considered his body as equipment he needed to do his job effectively, keeping it strong and honed for that reason. But now, with it coming alive under Daire's fingers, and Daire's glittering-eyed, open-mouthed appreciation scalding Gage's skin, he was happy for each swell and curve, every ridge, hollow and plane.

"Let me see you," he suddenly asked Daire, reaching for his shirt, wanting it gone, eager to see and touch the pixie's bare skin.

"In good time. First..."

That was all the warning Gage had before Daire slid lower, his clever fingers undoing Gage's pants and freeing his hard, heavy cock.

"What—? *Seriously*?" On his knees, Daire looked up through his tangle of hair, his eyes wide at what he was staring at.

Gage shrugged. Griffins' dicks were the biggest of the winged beasts', and he was, well, yeah, well-hung. Fine, *huge*. And bigger than usual now, throbbing with need, the head shining with pre-cum. His balls, heavy and full, were drawing up. But Daire didn't go for Gage's cock right away. The tormenting little pixie cradled Gage's balls, using both hands to cup the sac and a half-dozen fingertips to tap tiny beats on the sensitized flesh.

Gage cried out when his cock swung wildly, smearing streaks on his belly, and cried out louder when Daire lapped the smears up, his tongue velvet-rough on Gage's sensitive skin. "*Gods*," he ground out. "*Please, Daire.*"

"Please *Gage*, you mean. And I will," Daire promised. He shook his hair back and looked right into Gage's eyes, keeping their gazes connected even when he took hold of the base of Gage's cock and lowered his head. He barely paid attention to the head, just swiping his tongue over it to the tip and tasting the pre-cum there before he licked down the shaft, following a throbbing vein right to the base.

Gage grabbed for something—anything—to keep him on his feet, because his knees were wobbling, threatening to give out. He hollered when Daire rolled his balls in his hand and in one swift bob, sucked the aching tip of his cock into his mouth. Gods above, he'd never felt anything like that perfect heat and tightness. And had never experienced anything like when, a second later, Daire hummed around his dick…then sucked. *Hard.*

"*Daire,*" Gage tried to warn him. Warn him that the pleasure boiling and bubbling through him, as powerful and fiery as a volcano in the lava land of Planzatillo, had his climax erupting in seconds. Daire swallowed then swallowed some more until Gage's groans became cries because he was a shivering wreck, with nothing more to give. He pulled free of Daire's mouth, the perfection too much, and him now too sensitive, and Daire surprised and humbled him by kissing the softened tip as he let go.

Gage sank to the floor, facing him, unable to keep himself on his feet a second more, his new position bringing him down to Daire's level and close enough to curl a hand around the back of his neck to pull him in for a kiss. Daire, an eyebrow raised, kissed back, and Gage tasted himself on Daire's tongue.

That had Gage's eyes opening wide in surprise at the arousal that sparked to life in him again. How long would it take him to get hard again? Because he wanted more, wanted this handsome pixie he was clasping tightly. Stars in heaven, he wanted him, had a list of things he wanted to do with him, wanted Daire to do with him. To him. Would Daire…take him, in the way Gage wanted?

The thought of it had him curling his fingers into Daire's chestnut-brown mane and tightening them. Other images came on the wings of that one. Him, taking Daire's cock into his mouth, encouraging Daire to push into his throat, to lose control and fuck his face hard and furious until Gage choked. Him, spread out and tied down for Daire to explore, with his hands, his dick and…*toys*. Daire making him take everything he had to give, taking Gage to the edge again and again, until Gage was at his limits, and shifting into his griffin form with the sensory overload. Would Daire like him, in that form?

"Hey." Daire nipped Gage's bottom lip with his teeth, the slight bite of pain bringing Gage back from his musings. "Oh, I like that," Daire continued, and pinched Gage's nipples. Gage jolted, the sudden surprise and flare of pain making him throw his head back, which was when Daire bit his neck. Gage's gasp was loud.

Daire grinned, shifting to palm his erection. "So now what? You blow me and the first to recover fucks the other? Because I'm telling you now, those rumors about pixies' refraction time? *They're true.*"

Gage tried to reply but couldn't.

"What?" Daire reached out a hand and caught Gage's chin between his forefinger and thumb to study his face. Within seconds, a smile was tilting his lips. "Oh, I see. You like to bottom but… Griffin Guardians don't? Is that it?"

Something like that. The kingdom didn't care. Most griffins, the Guardians included, had sex with both griffins and she-griffins, but the corps had a more macho atmosphere, one Gage had come to maturity in. None of his fellow law enforcement troops bottomed, or if they did, didn't talk about it.

"Well, how about if it's our little secret that you like to get your ass fucked good? And, Soldier-Boy, I'm the best," Daire boasted. Then he dropped his braggart manner. "And I also nearly came when I was blowing you just now and squeezing that gods-made ass, so I'd really like to shoot my load while buried deep in it." He took one of Gage's hands and placed it over his erection.

Its thickness and hardness startled Gage and had his beak watering.

Daire gave a crooked smile. "Think that'll rub you up the right way?" he asked, standing — carefully — and stripping.

Gage had expected him to be pale, for some reason, but his body was as tan as it was wiry. His legs were longer than Gage had thought, and his cock… *Gods!*

"Better get your ass ready." Daire helped Gage to his feet and nudged him over to the bed, to lie on his front. Gage twisted his head to peer over his shoulder. "What?" Daire shrugged. "Told you I want my hands on that prime griffin rump."

Then he leaned down and ran his tongue from the top of Gage's crack to his asshole.

"*Fuck!*" Gage yelped at the feel of Daire's hot, wet tongue. He felt Daire's chuckle against his cheeks before the pixie pressed deep, laving with long laps. Gage writhed and squirmed, humping the mattress under him, his hole softening, the protector muscle giving way...for Daire to tickle his tongue tip inside.

This made Gage scream. He raised up and twisted his torso around when Daire backed away. Had he done something wrong?

"Lube," Daire threw over his shoulder, scrambling for his cloak and digging into inside pockets. "Mallow." He dragged out a small carved-root box.

"Mallow," Gage repeated. There were various kinds, all thick, tagmallow being the most common.

"Pepmallow," Daire specified, back behind him and one finger teasing a circle around Gage's pucker...before he pushed in.

"Pep...mal*low!*" Gage echoed in a voice that started as a roar and finished in a squeak. Pepmallow was —

"Warming. Like an itch deep inside..." Daire slid his finger in and twisted it to rub it over Gage's gland. "That you need to get fucked away." He pushed farther in and froze at the second bump. "What the blue skies? *Two?*"

His blood heating and his veins singing, Gage nodded. "Some...griffins...have another one. Hidden deep," he panted, then gave the longest, lowest moan in griffin history when Daire stroked there and *there*. He pushed back to bump Daire's unguent-covered fingers over those magic spots again.

"*Three?*" Daire gasped. "No fucking wonder you like to bottom. Jesus, I'd be offering my ass up to all comers."

Gage cried out when Daire twisted and turned his wrist, working his ass open. He was a griffin. They weren't known for begging, but *please* and *more* and *now* wanted to fall from his lips. "Daire," he ground out. "Fuck me."

"Oh yeah." Daire slid his fingers free to line up his cock and push in, slowly, forcing Gage's breath from his lungs in an agonized "Ohhh."

Daire's lack of speed, the way he rocked into Gage's ass an inch at a time, was driving Gage insane. He wanted hard, fast, relentless. Before he could voice his demands, Daire nipped into his neck, then his ear...still not powering in. He drew out slowly, his cock free of Gage for long, tormenting seconds, then thrust in.

"Take it by your screech that was what you wanted?" Daire whispered in Gage's ear. Gage's frenzied nod banged their heads together. Daire pulled out, fast, and this time drove leisurely back in, his cockhead scraping with slow deliberation over Gage's glands.

"Love the sounds you make for me," Daire told him. He pounded Gage powerfully and deep, maybe in reward.

Gage couldn't form a reply, not when liquid fire shot through him, making his balls fill and his dick stiffen, even though he'd come hard a few minutes ago. He twisted and Daire moved him so he was more firmly on his knees and could get a hand to his cock. Sun and moon, the arch of his back and neck—he was griffin shaped!

When Daire slid a hand up Gage's chest to pinch a nipple, Gage's ass clamped tight around Daire's cock. Gage barely needed the breathed "*Yeah*" in his ear to tell him another pinch was coming, but when Daire's wicked fingers made this one into a twist, it ripped a second climax from the base of Gage's spine, making him fuck his own fist while Daire plowed his ass.

The force of his release had him yelling his pleasure. Daire ceased his torment of Gage's nipple to grip his hips with both hands and give a last powerful thrust, tense, then climax, cum spurting from his dick in pulses that were longer than Gage's.

Gage stayed on his hands and knees as long as he could, then, his head ringing, he couldn't hold himself up any longer and flopped onto his belly.

He dislodged Daire, who pulled out fully and dropped beside him, both of them panting. After a minute or two, Daire levered himself up to look at Gage. "*Fuck,*" he breathed, his tone reverential.

Gage hadn't been expecting poetry or any kind of declaration, but this one-word reaction or assessment or whatever Daire had intended it as made him snort with laughter. "Fuck," he agreed.

"I think…" Daire dropped onto his back again. "That we should get our breath back, then see if we can find that third gland. Agreed?"

Gage tried to think how much time they had before they started the assignment tomorrow, but his brain gave up. *Gave in.* All he could do was echo the pixie.

"Agreed."

Chapter Eight

Daire's hum rippled into a purr and elongated into a moan, disturbing the silence of the morning bedroom. Hells and heavens, there was nothing like waking up to a blow job, sliding from sleep to half-wakefulness to full consciousness with tight wet heat engulfing his dick, making it grow along with his lazy arousal. *Oh yeah.*

He slipped free of the tendrils of slumber to raise his arm and pat where that mouth was sucking his cock. His hand landed on military-short hair. Blond hair, Daire knew without looking. And military short because his bed partner was a Griffin Guardian.

Gage. Daire let out a moan at a particularly good flick of Gage's tongue. Griffins had forked tongues...and it seemed Gage retained some residual ability of it when in his other form. Daire was going to take full advantage of it. He settled back with his arms folded under his head.

"Oh. You're just going to lie there?" Gage asked, pulling his mouth free and tipping his head back.

"No, I'll fuck you when you get me hard enough." Daire rolled his eyes at the idiocy of the question. Of course he'd tap Gage's tight ass. "So, go to." His mood buoyant, he tsked. "You just can't get enough, can you, griffin? Well, you know what they say, once you go pixie, you *go* pixie."

Gage muttered something about that not making any sense, just like Daire didn't, but Daire wasn't paying attention. He was too busy groaning at Gage's strong hand cupping his balls, then groaning once more when Gage licked the head of Daire's dick, his mouth as busy as his hand.

"Umm," Daire sighed — Gage took him deep. Well, it would only be polite to thrust. Just a few pumps into that heat and suction and...and Gage stopped.

"*Uhh*?" Daire grunted, wriggling at the tight band around the base of his shaft. Gage's hand? *What? Oh.* So the griffin wanted to play with him, did he? Wanted to be in charge of Daire's pleasure, bestowing it, bringing him to the edge of release, then stopping? "*Beast.*" Daire squirmed, trying to tempt Gage back onto his dick again.

"Winged beast," Gage boasted, bending to slide his mouth down Daire's shaft and removing the hand with which he'd kept Daire's release at bay. He jerked Daire in a couple of long strokes base to head, Daire's pre-cum and Gage's saliva giving him an easy ride.

That was more like it. Daire brought his legs up and let them fall open, tempting Gage with his asshole. Gage had fingered him nicely last night — or this morning. Daire tried to work out the time. Well, they didn't have to start their duties until ten of the clock. So yeah, he could go for Gage rubbing a mallow-lubed finger over his hole, then pressing *just* inside where so many nerve endings were, getting Daire writhing and sighing, then arching and moaning when Gage pushed deeper and added more fingers.

And earth and sky, those fingers stretched him as well as his favorite play-toys did.

Daire could see the scene already, him thrusting up to fuck Gage's throat and rocking back to fuck himself on Gage's thick fingers. All right, he'd let Gage play his power game, denying Daire his release—like now, sliding his lips free and ringing the base of Daire's cock. Oh, when Gage let him come, Daire was going to shoot his load in Gage's handsome face, leave that griffin dripping with pixie cum. Gage swallowing his release last night had been one of the sexiest sights Daire had ever seen, so this should be out of this realm.

Gage jacked him again, licking at the tip that emerged from his fist as if it were a holiday treat, some sugared sweetmeat, maybe. "Gage…" Daire said, trying to put a compulsion into his voice, because his whole body was tensed and his balls fucking *begging* for release.

"I know," Gage whispered. He coated one finger in the pre-ejaculate leaking from Daire's slit, and eased his hand down, to tickle that lubed fingertip around Daire's rim…then slipped it in.

"*Ahh*," Daire cried.

"Arrrgghh!" echoed from outside the small door in the far wall. "Arrrgghh!" It came a second time, followed by a long, wailing, "*Noooo!*"

The door, a connecting one, Daire now understood, burst open and an elderly, formally dressed male rushed in, one wrinkled hand to his chest and the other to his mouth. He removed the one from his mouth to point it, shaking, at the bed and its two occupants.

"Gage?" Daire asked. "Did you order up an old kook? Interesting thought, but—"

"She's *gone!*" cried the man. "*Taken!* And you, and you—you should have—were supposed to—and you...you—" He spluttered and shook too much to go on.

Daire raised bewildered eyebrows at Gage, who gave a puzzled head shake in reply. Whatever this was, it put an end to playtime. Daire wriggled and Gage's fingers slid free with a surprisingly loud *pop.* If his powers—well, the little he had—hadn't been stripped from him and most of the charms and spells he had about his person hadn't been confiscated, he'd have done his best to lay a pixie freeze on this intruder. He'd point at the intruder, focus all his intent—or was it intention? He hadn't studied much—and proclaim magic words.

"Shut up and stop shaking, you old fool!" he ordered, unable to bear any more...and the old fool froze where he stood, mid-gibber.

"What the deep hells?" Daire leapt from the bed. "Is he playing a joke? And who is he?" Reaching the man, which only took a few steps in this tiny room, he waved a hand in front of his face and when this got no reaction, poked him. The elderly...whatever he was had kind of solidified. He was still warm and alive, but unmoving, not breathing. like an effigy.

"Undo it!" Gage commanded, and Daire almost stumbled—Gage was in full uniform, looking not that much the worse for wear. "Unfreeze him! At once."

"I..." He didn't want to admit he couldn't, because he hadn't done it, hadn't frozen him. He sort of liked that Gage thought he had that level of pixie power. *He* liked the idea of having that amount of power. *Oh, the things I could do!*

Various scenes played themselves out in his mind. Him, eating and drinking all he liked at the Pixie's Neck while the tavern staff and customers were frozen in place. Him taking all he liked from the money-till at the Pixie's Neck and thumbing his nose at the security trolls. Him, patting Adam the Dwarf the landlord on the head—Adam hated that. Oh and hiding all the boxes and steps that Adam kept scattered about the place to stand on when he needed to be seen. *Oh, if only I had done this magic!*

Wait. Maybe he had? Whatever that Court shaman had done to him, he must have got it wrong, must have boosted Daire's abilities, such as they were, instead of nulling them! Goddesses' girdles! *Oh, I'm going to enjoy this!*

"It'll wear off," he said. These charms did, some sooner than others. Remembering the changeling charm he'd paid good money for—okay, well—had him frowning. "That squawking and twittering was..." He trailed off, watching Gage stride into the connecting room. It only took a glance, one Daire got as he pulled on his breeches and blouson, to see it was a much bigger room. *No, suite,* he found, hurrying in.

Gage's face had paled.

"Said you were a lightweight," Daire muttered, trying to figure out whose suite this was. *Someone really messy.* The bedlinen looked like it had been dragged off the bed, the chairs were overturned and a variety of items littered the floor. Gage rubbed his stomach. "You hungover?"

"I failed!" Gage burst out, searching wildly. "I lost the principal!"

"What, by enjoying some free time before we have to start work?" Daire asked. "That was betraying your morals? And may I remind you that you were enjoying it? A lot?" *Hypocrite.*

All these higher-being beasts were. Everyone knew that. Daire knew that. So why had he gotten involved with this one? This overly handsome, buff, blond, blue-eyed, huge-cocked one? *Oh yeah.* Daire gave a nod. He remembered.

"Prin-ci-pal," Gage ground out. "The person I was assigned to protect. She's gone."

"Hey, it's nothing to do with us if she arrived early and decided to go out for a little walk. See the sights of the capital. You know, the tavern. The racetrack. The tavern."

"You already said the tavern," Gage yelled, rifling through sheaves of parchment.

"There are two taverns!" Daire yelled back. "The Pixie's Neck and the Cockpit. So, she got here ahead of time and went out exploring." *Please,* he added silently, crossing his fingers behind his back and his toes in his boots.

"Only...she didn't. She got here on time according to her itinerary. Look." Gage grabbed the parchment off the floor and thrust it at Daire. "Her schedule. According to which, we should have been at work from ten of the evening yesterday, not starting at ten of the morning *this* morning." He glared at Daire as if it were his fault. "We should have checked the premises, the staff, done sweeps, patrolled —"

"And she's gone?" That old fart, her father or agent or whoever, had said so. He'd said *taken.* Oh, minatours' mucus and trolls' hairy balls, the state of the room sank in with Daire. "Gone as in *kidnapped*? Is there a note?"

"Not that I can see." Gage strode into the en suite bathroom,

"Who is it?" Daire asked.

"How should I know who did it?" Gage yelled.

"No, I mean who is she? The VIP you were guarding?"

"*We* were guarding." Gage returned, glaring at him.

"Fine. We." Daire acknowledged the correction.

"I assumed a keynote speaker." Gage started opening drawers.

"Huh. I thought singer, for the opening night, you know? All sparkly gown, sparkling vin, firefly lighting and —" Daire broke off at the World Magic Convention program Gage was holding out…turned to the page bearing a drawing of the guest of honor. "No. *No.*"

Jade, the Storm King, the leader of the Elves, stared back regally from the page, the tips of his pointed ears visible through his long black hair, the markings on his forehead clear. Oh, actually, Jade was also the Storm Queen, because royal blood meant he could and did change from man to woman. Jade, who'd recently married Grlind, the non-elf. The, well, *orc*. There was no other way of saying it. Grlind was a long-fanged, beady-eyed, overhanging-browed, lumpy, bald-pated pea-green orc. Who were famed for their violent, cruel, destructive natures.

"Gage…" Daire swallowed. "Tell me it's a Jade the Storm King tribute band playing at the opening ceremony. Or the closing. I'm not fussy."

"A what?" Gage demanded.

"The Storms. The Jades. The Kings," Daire invented wildly. "I can just hear the songs now. *When an Elf Loves*

an Orc. Forever your Elf. The Green Green Orc of Home."
Because if it was the ruler of the elf kingdom they
should have been keeping safe, and they hadn't, the
elves would— The orcs would—

Daire hurried back to the guy who'd interrupted
them. He studied the man's style of dress. As much as
he wanted to believe the stranger was wearing some
new style, something that even In The Closet didn't
stock, he couldn't fool himself. This was no pixie. It was
an elf. And if the occupant of the main suite had been
Jade, this must be one of her senior councilors.

Daire considered his options...and finished
dressing. In a hurry. He was swirling his half-cape
around his shoulders on his way to the door when Gage
came back in from the suite and caught him. "Where
are you going?" he demanded.

"I...thought I'd try getting through the Veil," Daire
replied, as if discussing a trip to the forest, to forage for
cogulumes and acorns. "Try my luck in the human
world, you know? There's an elf there now and a
wyvern. Well, they were recalled after the wyvern's
intestinal problems. Human food." He tsked. "Buffalo
wings, I ask you. Since when do buffalo have wings?
They have gills and fins!"

"Daire." Gage stood between him and the door.
"Apologies for asking, if I'm wrong, and I probably am,
but are you running away?"

"No-o-o!" Daire faked a laugh.

"In that case, I'm sorry." Gage gave a smart bob of
the head and clicked his heels together.

"Running away. Tsk!" About to lie, to say he was
getting kaffe and brot for their breakfast, Daire had an
attack of the truth. "I'm fleeing," he admitted.

Gage's face dropped, and Daire felt lower than a sand snake's scrotum. Since when had he cared what anyone thought about how he lived his life? "Oh, you think we should stay and face the music?" he scorned. "Well, I don't want to get the blame for someone else's screw-up. And I will. Pixie, remember? Lower being? Useless, brainless and all that?"

Gage didn't speak, just carried on with that tall, broad, smart-uniformed, looking-down-his-beak thing. No, worse. He looked disappointed. In Daire. Didn't he know Daire let everyone down, himself included?

"Look, come with me," Daire found himself saying. "We don't have to go through the Veil, but we should be anywhere but here. I'm not just thinking of my own skin." He was. Mainly. "You'll get fired, even imprisoned, or however griffins make a scapegoat of one of their own when there's been a foul-up and the race looks incompetent."

And it would be jail for him. Locked away from the sun and the wind and drink and food and games of chance. From everything that made life worth living. And trapped where his creditors and everyone else who had a beef with him would be able to find him. Might as well paint a big red target on his ass.

"And I'd decide quickly, if I were you," Daire added, seeing movement to his left. "Because that dried-up old stick that came with the Storm Queen? He's waking up."

Chapter Nine

"Argggh! Nooooo!"

Their visitor was unfreezing all right, and Gage could hardly think with the noise the elf was making as he did so. Well, okay, he wasn't thinking as much as berating himself. How could he have let this happen? He was a Griffin Guardian, with their motto *A mission undertaken is a mission accomplished*, not *A mission undertaken is a mission pissed against the wall*.

How? Because I was drinking and gambling and fucking like a pixie! Gage glared at Daire, unable to help noticing again the reds and browns in his hair and the glints of different greens in his eyes. He dragged his gaze to the other male, the one accompanying Her Highness. His hair was a mixture of silver and brown. Sal and pepp, they called that. Gage remembered seeing it when he was a gryphling.

"Sir," Gage began.

"She's —"

"Gone. You said," Daire finished for the courtier. They followed him back to the bigger room, where he darted about helplessly, and Daire leaned folded-armed in the doorway.

"Is there any chance she's just a bit messy? Used to servants cleaning up after her and all that? And popped out for a swift ale? They just got this weizen weissbier at the Cockpit, see, all creamy and tangy. Very refreshing. The whole town's talking about it. We got visitors come to the capital just to taste it! The Cock's on the outskirts, so a bit of a trek that takes its time, but one worth making." Daire nodded as if he'd solved the mystery. "That why you're early?" he continued. "Because you're not supposed to be here until later, right?"

"What?" the advisor screeched. "We're not early—we arrived as arranged *last night*." He thrust a few papers at Daire, who didn't take them. "And the Storm Queen is not 'messy' and is extremely unlikely to 'pop' anywhere for any alcohol, no matter how 'refreshing'." He lowered his voice. "Because the Storm Queen is with child!"

"Whose child?" Daire asked, then got it. "Pregnant? Ah." He pulled a face.

Waving his arms, the courtier turned on Gage. "And you, griffin, nothing to say for yourself? I'll have your wings and tail for this! And you..." He glared at Daire. "*Pixie*? Ha! That explains it all!"

Daire didn't react, but Gage didn't like the way this stranger spoke, the assumptions he made. "Daire the pixie is local liaison, yes," he said, keeping his temper. If anyone was going to yell at Daire and slap him about, it would be Gage. "Might I inquire, sir, why in her blessed condition, Her Majesty is—?"

"Gadding about the realm on a jolly?" Daire broke in. He lifted his cupped hand to his mouth and tilted it.

"Last night was Ladies Night at the Neck. Bar snacks, trivia quiz, cabaret, and they do Long Pixie Iced Teas half-price between sundown and moonrise. Alcohol and less-alcohol versions." He winked.

Their elderly visitor added jumping up and down on the spot to waving his arms. Gage couldn't quite understand all his reply, but got the gist, that the Storm Queen was scheduled to make a big speech about integration or equality of the species or something like that. Well, her councilor would know, Gage reasoned.

"And now this." The courtier turned slowly, taking in the room. "His Majesty's consort will—"

"Go orc?" Daire said.

Gage shushed him. This wasn't funny. When orcs got enraged, they destroyed, well, everything around them. Rooms. Buildings. Cities. "Grlind was made orc king, wasn't he?" he asked. He remembered the story, that Grlind had gone from outcast for refusing to slaughter a village—and yes, that was a village and not a villager—to ruler, after mating with the elven leader.

So in considering Grlind, they had the entire orc race to take into account too.

"When they get too deep into orc rage, they won't stop. Can't be stopped," Daire said. "Well, except by... You know."

Euthanizing. Gage did know. One of his first missions had been to put to death an orc that was gone too far into his rage to make it back. He'd been one of Gage's first kills, and one of the hardest.

"And then Her Majesty will die of grief!" the councilor wailed. "Elves mate for life and the Storm King being bonded to a mate of another species compounds that. Oh..." He clutched his middle. "I have a nervous stomach and any worry sets it off." His face was agonized.

"The bathroom's through there." Gage steered him across the room. As soon as the door was closed, he turned to Daire. "This is serious."

"Seems so." Daire winced at the noises coming from the en suite. "Hope there's enough paper."

"Quit acting the pixie," Gage ordered. "This is bad. However it happened, the person I should have been protecting has been kidnapped."

"So why's there no note?" Daire asked.

"Because they don't want anything." Gage had worked it out. "Anything other than what they've already got."

"The Storm Queen?" Daire took up the drawing. "And who's they?"

"Who stands to gain from the elven ruler being dead from grief at her consort euthanized? Or being unable to rule in general?" Gage asked, like he was an instructor teaching at the Guardian academy.

"Whoever's next in line, I guess," Daire answered. He frowned. "Weren't there some cousins?"

Gage nodded. He'd studied the background material provided as part of his assignment information. "Two male elves, Jaxon and Jaleb. They were banished from the elven kingdom for objecting to the ruler mating with another species. They've tried to become the figureheads for all the anti-interspecies protests. Probably stirred it up, to give them a way in if the Storm Queen was deposed."

"Crafty little elves!" Daire didn't sound as though he censured the traitorous pair all that hard. "And you think they came here and did this?" He indicated the room. "Because didn't you say something about this building winning an award?"

"It's got a ward!" Gage corrected, gritting his teeth.

"Yeah, I wasn't really listening," Daire admitted. "What? How could I, with you in front of me, all broad shoulders and crisp uniform and that *ass*?" He whistled.

"Stop thinking about my ass," Gage ordered.

"Stop flaunting it then." Daire shrugged.

"I'm not flaunting it!"

"Oh, please. The way that uniform's cut? It's *designed* to flaunt it." Daire rolled his eyes.

"It's —" Gage exhaled. This was getting them nowhere. Although knowing that Daire liked his ass — was getting them nowhere! "Only those who have business here can enter here," he said. "Meaning pixies. So…" He waited for Daire to put the pieces together.

"Right. Yep. Of course. Must be a pixie, because we're all scheming, good-for-nothing —"

Gage knocked aside the finger Daire was prodding him with. "Will you stop doing that! What I mean is, one or more pixies must be in league with Jaxon and Jaleb's plans. Not necessarily as pixies for hire. They could believe in the ideology the cousins are spouting." He didn't want Daire to think he held the usual prejudices against pixies. *Well…*

"What, all that 'purity of the races' stuff?" Daire didn't look convinced.

"We'll soon find out, when I question the staff." Gage was confident in his abilities. He was one of the best investigative Griffin Guardians in the corps.

They both jumped when the bathroom door opened, and the elderly courtier came out.

"Well, we'd better call in the militia," he said, one hand on his stomach.

"Sir." Gage stood straight. "I believe I can discharge my assignment and ensure the safety of the principal. Well, get her back, in this case. All I need is a little time."

"Time? If Her Majesty doesn't deliver her speech this evening, all hells will break loose!" The courtier wrung his hands.

"That's *hours* away. More than enough time!" Daire said, brightly. "Don't you worry, mister, we'll have her back here by then."

"Worry?" As if Daire had said a trigger word, the councilor shot back inside the bathroom.

"So that's agreed!" Daire called, shoving Gage from the room. "Come on then, Soldier-Boy, work your griffin magic. In a manner of speaking." He smirked.

Right. Gage would show him. Pulling his shoulders back and lengthening his stride, he strode into the admin offices, throwing his wings about, as was said of the Guardians.

"Every pixie? You want to see every pixie?" the director said in a squeak, at Gage's request.

He did. From reception to casino and every other nook and cranny in the convention center. And all in a line, puzzled though they might be, for him to march up and down in front of. "Now, you know what this is about," he barked and marched a little more, ignoring the shrugs and raised eyebrows as he did so.

"This way, they do the work for me," he said to Daire, in an aside. "Because the first to speak is always the guilty party." He whipped around at the sudden flurry.

"And the first to make a run for it?" Daire asked, pointing where the male pixie at the end of the line was bolting. "Would they be a guest at this guilty party too? Guest of honor, even?"

"Yes!" Gage hissed, giving chase. "Stay here, Daire. I'll handle this!"

"And miss this? I look like I floated down the Welling River in a bubble?" Daire shouted behind him.

Hellsapopping, Gage wished he'd studied the layout of the convention center so he knew it as well as the fleeing pixie seemed to. Then he would have been aware that this small room was the copy room, and maybe wouldn't have had reams of paper flung at him, fanning out through the air like malevolent white birds. Or bottles of ink hurled at him, staining his uniform with splotches of red, blue and green. He snatched up a wooden ruler and deflected a bottle of glue just in time.

"I hope they take this out of your salary!" he shouted at his opponent.

"Watch it!" Daire called, coming up fast behind him. "This corridor leads to the...kitchen," he finished, when Gage burst through the swing doors.

Gage wasn't quick enough to fend off the first egg, or the second or the third, and could hardly see through the haze of fine white spelt-wheat flour from the sack the pixie threw into the air and that caught on a light fitting, to burst open and rain down on them.

"Think you can cover your escape like that, do you?" Daire shouted.

"I'm trying!" the pixie shouted back, grabbing a big wooden jug.

"Watch the milk!" Daire warned, when a jerk of the pixie's hands had a wet white puddle spreading across the floor. "Hells' sirens, eggs, flour, milk—a few herbs and we've got an omell-lette! Now where's he gone?"

"Through there." Gage pointed at the small door…that led to a closet full of cleaning supplies, he discovered a second later when he tripped over a strategically placed broom and just dodged the bucket of disinfectant set up to fall on his head.

"You're making it worse for yourself, boy," he thundered, slipping and sliding on the floor wax that was glugging from the unstoppered container. Out through the closet's far door, in reception, Gage slowed a fraction to catch what Daire was doing behind him. He was beckoning pixies around and seemed to be—

"Are you laying odds on me catching him?" he shouted over his shoulder in disbelief.

"No!" Daire called back. "Well, if I'm honest, yes."

"How about helping me?" Gage roared, when the pixie sprinted for the doors.

"What, like I should work a sealing charm on the doors?" Daire asked. "Fine. Doors, be sealed. Now."

About to ask if that was it, because he could feel Daire rolling his eyes behind him, Gage clutched his stomach. Griffins didn't get sick, but they did need a lot of fuel and he hadn't eaten. But whatever Daire had done seemed to have worked, because none of his quarry's yanking and tugging at the center's doors did anything.

"Wow." Daire sounded astonished.

Trapped, the pixie turned to face them.

"Watch it, he's going to pouf," Daire warned.

"To…?" Gage didn't know the term.

"Pouf! Vanish," Daire explained, making a grab for the pixie. He was too late. With a puff of gray smoke, the pixie disappeared, there was a sizzling noise and Daire screeched.

"Daire! You okay?" Gage was at his side, his nose wrinkling at the burnt flesh smell.

"Ow! Trolls' shit and ogres' asses!" Daire shook his hand. "Whatever he was carrying, it was ferrous metal. Look." He held out his hand and a mark was burned into the flesh of his palm. "It'll heal. It's a pixie thing."

Ferrous metal... Gage knew little pixie lore but did know some couldn't stand the touch of iron. "Well, if you're not hurt, we should get to investigating that employee. Name, address, contacts..."

"No need. Not when we know where he likes to hang out." Daire blew on the mark.

It looked like two stylized letter Js, the wrong way round. He must have touched the thing upside down, Gage supposed.

"Because I know what this is," Daire continued. "It's a member token for a nightclub, the Double Jinx. It's a little... Well, let's just say I bet we'll find who's snatched the Storm Queen if we pay a visit there."

Chapter Ten

"And we can't fly there?" Daire whined again, hoping Gage would give in to his nagging instead of marching through the capital's streets, his longer legs making Daire rush to keep up. "Or is it all a lie about griffins and their...abilities?" If nagging didn't do it, maybe negging would.

Gage merely shot him a beaky look over one shoulder. "I offered you a ride," he reminded Daire.

"Been there, done that," Daire muttered. And while he wouldn't say no to another fuck, Gage was all eyes-front-shoulders-back, duty, duty, duty. *Probably pretending it never happened. And why wouldn't he?* Daire had screwed up as usual. *Screwed and screwed up.*

"Yes, I know that's not what you offered," he said, before Gage could. He had no intention of taking Gage up on his offer to carry Daire on his shoulders, no matter how broad and strong they were. "We don't want to reinforce stereotypes now, do we?"

Daire was still puzzling over how he'd sealed the center's doors. He could never work magic like that!

That shaman must have really screwed up and given him the magic he'd removed from all the sentenceds that day! Maybe he could get Gage to fly them across town to the club, after all, with a little bit of persuasion. Well, compulsion. *Same thing*, Daire reasoned, focusing on Gage a little ahead of him.

Gage stopped, rubbing his stomach.

"You okay?" Daire caught him up.

"Think I need to eat," Gage replied, straightening up. "I don't want to stop, when we should be working the case, but..."

He must take a lot of feeding. Daire forced himself to hold back the words that rose to his lips, that he had something the griffin could eat. He looked around. They were past the market, just by the main square. "Yeah, let's get breakfast. We got time and here's okay."

"Pixies Pantry?" Gage looked at the kiosk Daire led him to.

"I know. It's nothing like *my* pantry. Go sit. Oh, and give me some money." Daire helped himself from Gage's pocket and shoved him over to one of the tree stump tables with their matching seats. He waited in line for two pannkakes with the works and a couple of sides.

"Bangers and bakon," he said, identifying the items for Gage as he placed the plates down. "With domates."

"They're...red." Gage took up a fork. "And that salchise thing...is black?"

"Erm, yeah?" Daire shoveled a forkful of pannkake in and sliced the blodbanger into thin discs while he chewed. "If you can't eat it, I will." Not everyone liked things made with blood, and Gage probably ate fresh fruit and drank powdered jinja root in hot water of a morning.

"And this yolk is yellow." Gage smeared it onto his fried spelt-wheat bread. "Eggs. Do they have a crazy name here?"

"Yeah. Egges." Fighting an eye roll, Daire flicked a few slices of blood salchise onto Gage's plate for him.

Gage was soon wiping his plate with the last bit of his pannkake. He sat back, the koffi cup looking small in his big hand, and studied Daire. "Why did you agree to this liaison work?" he asked suddenly. "You don't strike me as the volunteering sort."

"What, not wanting to do my bit to serve my people?" Daire dabbed at his mouth. "Of course I would, when it was either that or prison."

"Prison?" Gage set his cup down.

"I'm not exactly a model citizen, if you hadn't figured it out already. And this was my last chance, okay? And what about you?" Daire prodded. "Seems to me this bodyguarding wasn't your usual kind of mission either."

"I...well... Yeah. It was this or suspension," Gage admitted. "I disobeyed orders."

"All right!" Daire clapped. "Go, you! Oh, you mean you filled something out in duplicate and not triplicate? In blue ink and not black?"

Gage laughed. "It's getting like that. All the rules and orders, you know? I...used excess force. Among other things."

"No! Tell me!"

Gage did and Daire listened open-mouthed to the tale. *Gage isn't totally the uptight by-the-book law enforcement officer he might think he is. Might want to be.* Daire smiled. He and Gage weren't that different, under the skin. And fur. And feathers. He realized he was very curious about Gage's other form.

"Magic users. Can't say I like them." Gage gave a shudder as he finished. "Come on. Let's get this job done and things back on track." He frowned. "Wait. A club, you said? Doesn't that mean it won't be open yet?"

"Not exactly." Daire steered him around the corner. "Not open to the public yet, yeah, but to those in the business..."

Gage took in the line of people that stretched from the door to halfway along the street, his gaze going from the trio of identical girl dancers to the male contortionist. "They're here to audition? To be acts in the club?"

"No. *We* are," Daire replied, marching them both to the doors. "Look, we have to play it crafty. You can't just burst in. You don't have jurisdiction here."

"But I'm a damn Griffin Guardian!" Gage roared, standing tall and proud.

"Ooh, *like* it!" lisped a male pixie with a large double J on his clipboard.

"You in charge?" barked Daire. "My boy doesn't wait in line, see. Not when he's only in the Lands for a limited amount of time. He's the opening act at the convention, and looking to demo his new moves, see." He chomped on a cigarillo from his pouch in his role as an agent.

"But—" Gage started, then hopped and hopped more when Daire stood on the toes of one foot then another.

"*Really* like it!" The club pixie gave a tiny handclap at Gage's dance. He took a sly peep around. "Now, I shouldn't do this, but I will. I'm going to push you to the front of the audition line!"

"*What?*" burst from Gage.

"Oh no. No no no no no." Daire tsked a little as he shook his head. "My boy don't *audition*. He *performs*." He stuck another cigarillo in the pixie's mouth.

"Really?" The club pixie spat out the cigarillo. "He's that good? I mean, he's got the face. And the bod." He walked in a tight circle around Gage. "Front and back…"

A pang of jealousy shot through Daire at this idiot admiring Gage's tight buns.

"What…?" Gage flapped his hands at the pixie. "I'm not a slab of meat! I'm a Griffin Guardian!"

"Were." Daire jumped in. "Still, federal law enforcement's loss is the world of entertainment's gain, eh?"

Another older pixie came out of the club, his eyes narrowed, and Daire, used to reading people, pricked up his ears. "As I say, my boy needs to demo his new moves. So, how about he performs here for one day only — for free? Oh, headlining, of course."

"Sold!" said the older pixie, shaking both their hands at once.

The other pixie squealed in delight. "Go right on through," he urged them, opening the doors. "And the artist will make your picture, for the poster!"

"See?" Daire said out of the side of his mouth as Gage was ushered into a small room to pose for the house artist. "I got us in, didn't I?"

"Yes. And there's only one problem." Gage looked from the artist's glossy, bold depiction of him on stage, to Daire and gulped. "I…can't actually dance."

* * * *

"You can't dance. You can't *dance*. You could have told me that before I got you the gig!" Daire shouted, waving his arms around inside the private dressing room he and Gage had commandeered.

"I could have, yes…if you'd told me your plan!" Gage waved his arms in reply. "But no. You go off half-cocked, or actually, full-cocked and — Stop sniggering!" he ordered.

"Stop saying cock then," Daire got out through his sniggers. "Look, I was improvising, okay?"

"Are all pixies like this?" Gage paced the room. "Like their reputation?"

That hurt, a little. "We have commandments. Regulations," Daire answered, stiffly. "A Guild."

"To control the magic." Gage spoke like one who'd read some official documents on his way to the Lands. "And I thought you got a hench animal, from the Guild, to assist you?"

"A hench? Yeah, we do."

"A slyfox, a crooked rook, a caterwaul, a black dog…" Gage named the top henches. "I've never seen yours. Where is it? What is it?"

Part of Daire wanted to lie, to invent some wondrous beast, but he didn't. "Here. In my pocket. I got a snoremouse." He pulled out the tiny sleeping creature that was the size of Daire's thumb, and it snuffled and twitched, swiping at its eyes and ears with a titchy paw. Daire scowled. "Meet Fang."

"Good scary name."

Fang's whiskers fluttered.

"Yeah, well. He doesn't do much," Daire admitted in a whisper.

"He's…cute." Gage stroked its tiny nose. "I can't see him helping you much, though?"

"Reason I stopped paying my dues to the Guild. And I probably got him because the ones I did pay, I paid in false coin," Daire admitted. People had tried to tell him he created a lot of his own problems, but it hadn't sunk in until now, with Gage looking at him like that. "Look, about the dancing. You can probably manage all right. Show me what you can do."

Daire took his pfeife and got a tune going, adding hand drumbeats to it. A simple charm got the music going while Daire studied Gage's dancing. *Is that dancing? He's not having some sort of full-body spasm?* Whatever it was, it was painful. He'd told the truth. He couldn't dance.

"Stop," Daire begged, unable to bear the scarecrow on a pole-type flailing about any longer. "Like this. Copy me. Stand legs apart. Click fingers, shake fingers."

He demonstrated, shaking his hands at his sides. He enjoyed dancing. He'd picked up some good partners line dancing in the Cockpit. "Knee tap. Foot tap. Hands on hips. Round the world with your pelvis," he instructed.

"Oh, come on!" Gage glared

"Side cross. Other side cross. Then turn and point. And try not to look like you're facing a firing squad. Spin. Cross arms. Move arms up, move arms down. Try to look sexy here? And thrust…"

Gage wasn't thrusting.

"Maybe lick your lips?" Daire suggested. "Without the death glare?"

This wasn't working. Daire stood next to him, their hips touching. "Try again?" It wasn't much better.

"Stand behind me," Daire said, "and feel the movements I make. Maybe that'll be easier?"

It was…harder. As in Gage's hard erection pressing into Daire's ass. Unable to stand it — he was only pixie, after all — Daire twisted around, bringing them face-to-face, and cock to cock. This time when he thrust his crotch, Gage thrust his too, and they ground together.

"Is this dancing or foreplay?" Gage whispered.

"Aren't they the same?" Daire replied, sliding his hands down to Gage's backside and squeezing. Heat and lust fired through him at the feel of that taut ass, and he climbed Gage, wrapping his legs around the griffin's waist so he could rub more thoroughly.

And Gage rubbed back, just as thoroughly. He moaned, his eyes a bright sky blue as he stared into Daire's. It wasn't enough, and their clothes were in the way. How could Daire feel that hard body with Gage clothed like this? How could he bite into those tiny, tight nipples with the uniform tunic covering them? And, moving lower, how could he take Gage's rock-hard cock in his mouth, with him wearing those pants?

"Gods. What you do to me," he gasped.

Gage looked startled. "I was just about to say that!" he replied. "I've never been like this before."

"Like what?" Daire asked but prevented Gage from replying by kissing him.

"Like…" Gage pulled his lips free. "This! Wanting someone I barely know to throw me down and take me! Have his way with me. Hard. Leave me aching."

Daire groaned. He felt the same way, needing Gage beneath him, his muscular legs drawn up, exposing his perfect pucker to Daire, who would worship it. His hand was on their fly buttons when a tap came at the window, then another, then a squawk.

"Shit!" Gage pulled free and sprang to open the window...to the green and blue papagai rapping on it with its beak. He shook the bird's claw, his manner formal.

"Status report?" demanded the bird in a screech.

"Fine. Yes. Fine. Yes. I liaised with the principal's handler." Gage nodded. A lot.

Interesting. It was always useful to know a person's tells when they were not being wholly truthful. Daire grinned.

The bird repeated the message back, squawked again and left.

"Okay. That?" Daire asked, puzzled.

Gage sighed. "I have to file reports. We use a papagae network. They relay the message from one to another and back to my commander, and pass anything along to me."

And kill the mood. Well, the noise outside indicated that the place was filling, the Double Jinx's clients there for the lunchtime opening. What brought them here all day? Daire knew what made the most popular acts...popular. He eyed Gage. "Let's try again. But with a modification." He clicked his fingers at Gage. "Get that uniform off."

"I don't understand," Gage replied, nevertheless wriggling out of his tunic and pants.

Daire took up a pair of scissors and started cutting into the pants. That done, he took up a packet of snap fasteners.

"You will," he said, with a wink. "You will."

Chapter Eleven

"I can't do this." Gage grabbed at Daire. He never admitted to fear or doubt, and considered the impossible a jumping-off point, but now, standing in the wings, waiting for his turn to take to the stage... "I. Can't. Do. This," he repeated, clutching Daire hard.

"Course you can! You have to, because we need an excuse to stick around, remember?" Daire lowered his voice and pulled them away from the other acts. "Seeing as your attempt a little earlier to find out information didn't get us anything."

Fine, maybe it hadn't been the best idea to march into the communal dressing room and shout, "*Any elves here? I want to interrogate any elves here.*" But he'd wanted this over with, wanted to move the assignment on. "Sorry," he muttered.

"I think we got away with it."

Daire had faked a laugh and said something about Gage trying to introduce comedy into his routine. "*Stick to the sexiest dancing in the kingdom act,*" he'd said.

"*I doubt that,*" one of three identically dressed male pixies had sneered. Three identically dressed in fishnet stockings and high-heels male pixies.

Gage looked across at the three now. Killer Heels, they were called, and they had stiletto shoes. Literally — their heels were blades. He suspected they might be assassins. "I should go arrest that trio," he decided, turning to go do exactly that.

Daire grabbed him. "Look, I'll give you something to help," he whispered. He took a small wooden box from his pouch and unscrewed the lid. "It's pixie wishing dust. See?"

Gage bent to see, and Daire blew some into his face, then muttered an incantation Gage couldn't catch or understand. It sounded like nonsense to him, but what did he know? Daire's face was close to his. *Close enough to kiss.*

"Gods, you're sexy," Daire hissed. "Now, get out there and dance. The moon-sparkle powder will fill you with the power of the moon and make you shine."

"Moon-sparkle powder? It's not pixie wishing dust?" Gage asked.

"Oh, right. Well, it has various names." Daire didn't meet his eyes as he put the box away. "I'll be at the center front table, remember, so you can copy me."

"And now, the plane's sexiest griffin shifter...Hot Wings!" yelled the MC.

"Go!" Daire's push coincided with the music starting and Gage found himself on stage. *Shit. Hells.* Where was Daire? Right there, starting the moves they'd worked out, his eyes on Gage, who stared back, right into that entrancing green gaze.

"*Dance for me.*" Gage heard, as if Daire had spoken, and he did, moving to the song playing as though he'd been dancing to it from hatchhood. Turn, spin, point, cross, lick lips — the crowd were on their feet, whistling and clapping.

Daire mimed shrugging off his blouson, and Gage, understanding, tore off his tunic. The crowd cheered. The next move was the pants. "*Tease the audience,*" Daire had instructed, so Gage did, making a big deal of undoing his belt and flicking the ends where he let them hang before whipping the leather strip away.

He threw it into the audience and Daire leapt up and caught it before anyone else could. It was then Gage realized who he was dancing for — Daire. It was Daire whose eyes he stared into when he grabbed the hips of his pants and tugged, pulling the legs away to leave him in booty shorts. It was Daire's heart Gage wanted to fill with lust, when he turned around and wriggled his ass at the crowd — an ass that was shown by the cutouts in the shorts.

Gage didn't plan what happened next and didn't even realize what had happened until he felt something sweeping then waving behind him and heard the crowd roaring — his tail was there and out, bobbing to the music. He spun to face the audience and Daire, and first one wing, then the other manifested, beating the air in time to the raunchy music playing. Ear-splitting yells and stamps of feet filled the place.

"Tal-*ons*, tal-*ons*," screamed the clubgoers and Gage obliged, stretching out one hand to pop out his claws from it, then the other. He wasn't looking at the audience, though. All his attention was on Daire, who was looking back at him, his mouth open and the bulge in his pants almost as huge as Gage's.

The music and the audience's applause reached a crescendo. Gage gave a final turn, a last wriggle of his ass, a closing lash of his tail, and fled the stage, panting, his heart thudding. Daire was waiting, his hands on his hips, and looking as though he had a lot to say about Gage's display. *Good.* That was why he'd —

All thoughts dissolved when Daire flung out a hand, grabbed Gage by the back of his neck and yanked him down to kiss him, his mouth hard on Gage's and his tongue dominating. He pulled his mouth free and demanded, "What was that? I told you to dance and shine, not sex the whole club up!"

"What was that? That's what I want to know!" Gage shouted back. "That... I don't... Did you sprinkle me with an aphrodisiac by mistake? You're not the most organized of pixies, after all."

"Of course not!" Daire snapped.

Gage wriggled. "What's that? Stirring in your pants?"

Daire scoffed. "We've already established what you do to me."

"No—in your pocket!" Gage pointed. "It's your hench."

A tiny black nose tip poked itself out, the rest of the snoremouse's head following, just as two tiny paws gripped the pocket.

"Fang?" Daire poked him. "He never wakes up. Well, only when there's danger. Like, when enemies are...here..."

Shouts and screams rang out from the club.

"Daire the pixie!" yelled a voice. "Daire the no-good, cheating pixie—I know you're here! And I have got two balls!"

"Always good to have. And good to know," Gage remarked. "Friend of yours, the two-baller?"

"Monops," Daire sighed. "Long story."

"You cheated him," Gage guessed.

"Oh, apparently not that long." Daire tried a grin.

"Come and face me!" Monops ordered.

"What? No!" Daire grabbed at Gage's waistband, but Gage was already striding out onto the stage. "This is a bad idea!" Daire hissed behind him.

The club was even more full than it had been.

"I got more people here want to have a word with you." The pixie in the eyepatch grinned, indicating other men who looked just as happy to see Daire.

"Don't look at me like that," Daire ordered Gage. "My medical issues got me into debt, okay?"

"Really?" Gage took the measure of the cutthroats and villains advancing.

"Yeah. I'm addicted to betting. Wind-hounds, kamels, water fairies...I can't pass an oddsmaker without making a wager." Daire gulped.

"You suffer from addiction?" Gage asked.

"Well, not so much suffer as enjoy, really," Daire admitted. "Mostly..."

He indicated the approaching thugs and the massive bird-like animal that was swooping low over the terrified crowd. Its wingspan had to be twenty feet across — and the wings were skin, membraned, not feathered — and its head large on its long neck. Its beak was as sharp as its hooked claws. It dipped low enough to touch a male pixie in the audience with the tip of its wing, and the pixie's scream, filled with horror and anguish, almost deafened Gage.

"What the stars is that?" he gasped.

"A terror-dactyl," Daire answered. "It touches you, and it's like you're living in your worst fear."

"Now, that's a hench." Gage nodded, then cried out at the nip to his finger. He looked wildly about and caught the tip of a brown tail vanishing inside Daire's pocket. "Your snoremouse bit me!" he exclaimed.

"Never mind that. Come on!" Daire turned for the wings.

"You're fleeing?" Gage couldn't believe it. He wanted to stand his ground against the shouting, threatening mob.

"No, *we're* fleeing!" Daire grabbed him and yanked him along. "If you get into trouble here, your commander will know what's happened. He'll recall you, and we'll never be able to solve the case."

"But where are we going?" Gage tried to slow Daire's flight, but the pixie was strong.

"This way." Daire pulled him outside, the shouts of his enemies showing they were following. "Here, in fact."

"The steeds?" Gage looked from the line of horses tied to the railing outside the club to Daire.

"Can you think of a better way to escape?" Daire retorted. He ran past the valet pixie and stopped at the second section of steeds.

"Sirs, you can't—" the valet started, trying but failing to stop Daire leaping on the back of a dappled gray. Daire struggled to unhitch the reins from where they were tied to a post and after a second, took out a pocketknife and cut through the leather straps.

"But that's—" the valet began.

"Gage, get on!" Daire cut the valet off. As soon as Gage was astride the steed, Daire yelled, "Yah! Away!"

The horse obeyed, taking them away—in the form of up.

"—a flying horse!" the valet finished, from below them on the ground.

"Figured that out by the wings," Gage muttered, shifting around to avoid being clobbered about the head by the pair of gray wings that had unfolded from the horse's withers and that were flapping in between him and Daire. "Daire—"

"Shh! I'm trying to figure out the controls!" Daire snapped. He flicked the sawn-off reins about and all he succeeded in doing was making the beast fly in a circle.

Gage took a look at the shouting, weapon-waving, fist-shaking mob below, who all seemed to think Daire was mocking them, in doing these victory laps. He ducked to dodge the various missiles hurled skyward at them.

They were still over the club, and Gage considered the venue. He'd had no chance to carry out an investigation, of course, but from the short time he'd been there, and what he'd observed, it didn't seem the kind of place he and Daire were seeking.

It had been full of pixies intent on having a good time, or pixies who made a living supplying a good time to those seeking it. No one had seemed political, and the more he thought about it, the club seemed an unlikely hotbed of sympathy with causes of another kingdom. He glanced at the club's logo gleaming on its roof.

"Those double Js are different to your burn," he commented, recalling the mark that had scorched Daire's skin, but that was now faded to nothing.

"It was upside down," Daire reminded him, then screeched when the horse rolled over in the air. "Not you, nag! Upright, upright!"

"This is crazy." Gage had barely clung on. "You know I fly, yes?"

"Yeah. And I can't wait to see you." Daire looked over his shoulder, licking his lips.

"Oh, horseshit." The horse turned its head too and rolled its eyes as it looked at them. "You're not gonna make out on my back, are you? I hate it when passengers do that. Makes me heave." He gave a heave, in demonstration, almost dislodging them.

"It…he…you…speak?" Gage asked, feeling stupid.

"Costs you extra, but yeah," the horse replied. "What d'ya need, guided tour? Info on where to go in town?"

"I'm no tourist!" Daire shouted.

"Then why ya here?" The horse snorted down at the club.

"We were looking for a place with a double J symbol, but upside down. The symbol, I mean," Gage replied, feeling that his life had been upside down since he'd stepped foot in the Pixies Lands.

"Not a place!" the horse harrumphed in disgust. "And it's not even local. The reverse double Jule is the symbol of revolution in the elf kingdom. The group that's against the Storm King."

"How do you know?" Daire gasped. "And fly onward, please."

The horse snorted but shot forward. "Cabby, remember? We know everything."

"Really." Daire scooted forward. "Then do you know who's likely to kidnap the Storm King?"

"Them cousins, duh." The horse shook its mane.

"And where would they take her—him?"

"Daire…" Gage didn't think it was good to reveal too much.

"Where all kidnap victims get taken, no matter what kingdom they get snatched from." The horse looked down. "We're nearly at the capital limits. I'm not going south of the creek, not at this time of day."

"And what place would that be, where victims are taken?" Daire prodded.

"Gods' sake, over the rainbow!" The cabby-horse shook his head at their ignorance.

"Of course!" Daire echoed.

"What? The sunlands?" Gage almost slipped off and gripped the horse tighter, making it whinny. "You mean she's *dead*?"

Chapter Twelve

"Wet behind the ears, this one," the horse-cabby commented, descending a little.

"Am I?" Gage felt behind one. He was sweating, yes. More so now with that news. If the Storm King was dead, had been killed —

"No. Over the rainbow is a place." Daire grabbed at the horse's mane against the drop. "It's organized crime's hideout region. A place where criminals or exiles go to relax, don't commit any crimes and bring their money."

"The premier destination for the global criminal elite," the horse said.

Neither sounded as though this was a bad thing. Gage was about to ask if the horse would take them there, but the speed at which the ground was approaching suggested otherwise.

"Have to let you out here, gents," the cabby said, rising in the air on his hind legs.

"So by let us out, you mean tip us off," Gage commented, sliding over the horse's rump and falling a few feet to the ground. Daire had farther to slide and slip, and Gage broke his fall for him. "Could you send your bill to the Griffin Guardians HQ?" he asked the cabby. "I'll give you the assignment number."

"Sure." The horse repeated it back once Gage recited it. "Well, don't let me stop you giving me a tip..."

Both Gage's and Daire's search for coins came up empty. "Sorry," Gage apologized.

"Not a problem. Turn around." The horse, flapping its wings to stay airborne, made a circle motion with its head. "Not you, shorty," he said when Daire went to move. "Just the blond. Slowly..."

Bewildered, Gage spun in a slow circle.

"Nice. I'd spread butter on those buns and lick it off," the cabby praised.

"Pervert!" Gage exclaimed, clutching his rear.

"Me? I'm not the one wearing cut-off shorts with my ass hanging out of them, am I, sweetcheeks?" the horse asked, and flew off, neighing.

"Fair enough," Gage had to admit. He focused on his uniform and got it back to Guardians' standard. "Right. So, we have to get to this rainbow place. How?"

"It's at the edge of the Pixies Lands. Well, the edge of all lands, I suppose." Daire pointed. "And we'll need a leprechaun as a guide, to get us over."

"Oh!" Gage had heard of them, of course. "You stalk them, and catch them by the neck and squeeze tight, right?"

"Fuck, no!" Daire looked appalled. "You hire one! They hang out there for clients."

"And we have to get there as quickly as possible." Gage looked about. No one seemed to be around. "Stand back," he ordered, moving back himself when

Daire didn't get out of the way quickly enough. In the blink of an eye, he was in griffin form.

Gods and goddesses, sun, moon and all the stars — Gage was a beautiful griffin. Fine, so Daire had only ever seen one in the distance before and for all he knew, they were all well-made and handsome, but Gage was *beautiful*. It could have been an odd mixture, a creature with the head and front legs of an eagle and the body, hind legs and tail of a lion, but both beasts were regal, powerful and ruled their kingdoms, so the blend had both species' majesty and strength.

The grays and blacks of the eagle's feathers shaded somehow into the tawny and sands of the lion's coat. How would the spring of the feathers feel, especially when they became the thickness of the fur? Gage bobbed and bent, and, understanding, Daire threw a leg over Gage and sat astride him.

He'd thought Gage combined sky and earth before, in having feathers and pelt, but *understood* it now, from flying on his back high in the air. Daire slipped a hand behind him, to spear his fingers into the silky pelage, and curled the other — gently — around plumage, experiencing both at the same time. Their feel made him exclaim out loud. Gage wriggled under him.

"Oh, straight on. Then left." Because Gage was asking for directions, wasn't he? It was logical. Just as logical as how having Gage between his thighs, in whatever form, had Daire's balls tightening. Gage purred, or rumbled, and the sounds rolled right through Daire. He felt it, from the base of his neck and down the length of his spine, and when it settled, his arousal grew almost to the point of pain.

"Here. Here's fine," Daire gasped out when they were over the hinterland, as if he were directing an actual cabby, and Gage swooped lower, his descent a lot smoother than the horse's had been. The moment Gage touched the ground, Daire stumbled off. "You..." At a loss for words, he raised a hand and sliced it across the air, mimicking the shape of Gage's griffin form. "I want to feel you all over, but now..."

Gage seemed to understand. A heartbeat, and he was in his other form once more, sitting naked on the ground. His position made it easy for Daire to push him onto his back, and dive on top of him. "You sexy fucker. Got me so horny for you," Daire ground out, rolling them onto their sides.

He wriggled around until he lay with Gage's dick in his face. It stiffened as he breathed on it, and Daire jacked it root to head, his fingers tight around the swollen length. He fumbled his own free of his breeches, and Gage immediately fisted the base of it. "Taste me," Daire growled, and Gage obeyed, licking from right above his hand to the tip.

"Yes," Daire hissed. "Suck me, griffin."

Under him, alongside him, Gage shuddered and opened his mouth. He blew on the head of Daire's cock and lapped at the slit. Daire shivered. This wasn't enough. He made enough space to rip his breeches and boots from his legs, then hooked a leg around Gage's neck.

"I said suck me," he demanded, pushing his crotch into Gage's face.

Gage let himself be pushed. He opened wide, tearing a groan from Daire. Daire thrust hard, too shaky with arousal to start slow and gentle, to build up gradually. His force had Gage gulping and gagging, and Daire pulled free. "You okay?" he gasped.

Gage's nod bumped him into Daire's rock-hard erection. "Fuck my face," he whispered.

Daire gave as much of a smile as he could, given his aching dick. "Oh, I will," he assured Gage. "And you'll take everything I give. Every rough, hungry thrust." He powered back in, taking Gage's cock into his mouth at the same time, making Gage moan around his own mouthful. Daire was too far gone for teasing or playing. He sucked hard and flicked his tongue around Gage's fat length.

Gage cried out. Their movements synchronized, and Daire knew the pleasure flickering through him like fire was burning Gage from the inside out too. That understanding doubled the pleasure, stoking it with each strong suck, each tongue flick and each caress of the other's balls.

Then it was Daire's turn to moan. He fucked Gage's mouth faster, chasing the climax that was building in him. Gage was keeping pace with him, or Daire was bringing him along with him, and the agonized cry Gage gave, one that vibrated around Daire's cock like thousands of tiny hairs, was high with pain then lower with relief when he jetted down Daire's throat.

Daire didn't think he'd ever come as hard in his life as he did then, pumping into Gage. Gage gagged again, but kept up the tight seal of his lips, the rippling of his throat, drinking Daire down, just as Daire took care to swallow every drop of Gage's spunk, and lick every smear away when he pulled his mouth free. He had to force himself to slide his softened dick from Gage's mouth—he would have left it there until Gage got him hard again, but that wasn't possible.

"What?" Gage rasped.

"We're being watched," Daire mouthed, giving a jerk of his head to the left where a scuffling in the undergrowth and the waving of the leafy bush had caught his attention.

A slight nod and the narrowing of Gage's blue eyes told Daire the griffin understood. Gage looked furious, as if he should have been aware of an interloper, should have guarded against it or protected Daire from it. He was a soldier, after all.

Gage rolled and leapt to his feet, clothed in a second and darting for the bushes. Daire admired his strength and agility. He wanted to stretch out, luxuriating in how sucked dry his balls felt and how his dick was still twitching with aftershocks. *Fuck*, Gage gave good head. He hoped Gage thought he did too.

But no. No chance to rest. Not when an indignant piercing screech came from the undergrowth, and the entire line of bushes shook with the struggle that was going on.

"Got one!" Gage shouted. "Daire, I got— *Ow*! That hurt!"

"Oh, they fight back," Daire yelled, over the thuds and thumps. He pulled on his breeches and was stamping into his boots when Gage backed out of the greenery, dragging a small struggling creature.

A leprechaun.

"Get your fat hands off me, ya fucking gobshite!" it ordered.

A demanding, foul-mouthed leprechaun.

With a guttural, "Ya shitehole!" it kicked out at Gage's shins.

A demanding, foul-mouthed, violent leprechaun.

"But I captured you!" Gage told it. "I have the right to—"

"You have the right to bite the back of me fucking bollocks, ya lickshite," the leprechaun interrupted. It dangled in the air, its limbs flailing where Gage held it by the back of its coat collar. Its rusty-red beard was almost as long as its body, which, okay, wasn't that long, and its bald head had been burned to a dull red-brown in the sun. Its face looked like a furious potato.

"I thought you granted wishes!" Gage protested.

"Oh yeah, I do…if your wish is a good beating with me shillelagh," the creature retorted. "I'd like you to feel its knob."

Daire looked at Gage and Gage looked back, both of them a little open-mouthed. "Your…what?" Daire asked.

The leprechaun wriggled its arm inside its long coat and pulled out a stout wooden walking stick, like a cudgel, with a large knob at the top, in answer. He brandished it, until Gage grabbed it from him.

"Take this." He passed it to Daire.

"Yeah, take it and shove it up yer—"

"Gag him. And tie him up," Daire advised, cutting the leprechaun off. "I'll help."

"Get off on this, do ye?" the creature mocked as they looped vines around him, fastening him to a tree.

"Sometimes," Daire admitted. He doubted this would be one of them, though. He shuddered at the thought. The leprechaun smelled like a mixture of trolls' nuts and ogres' armpits.

Their task done, Gage beckoned Daire away. "What now?" he asked.

"Don't know," Daire admitted. "I've only heard tales about them. I don't actually *know* much about them."

"I can fucking hear you, you lickasses!" the creature yelled, still struggling. "Come here and learn all about me. I'll learn you the bones from your bodies, so help me!"

"Maybe he'll trade a wish for his release?" Gage suggested.

He was sure fixated on the 'leprechauns grant wishes' idea. Daire tried to let him down gently. "I don't think that's how they work."

"Then maybe we have to use his weaknesses against him?" Gage nodded, then strode back to the tree that held their captive. "Look here," he said, pulling his badge from his pocket and brandishing it in the leprechaun's face. "This amulet will turn you to stone."

Daire closed his eyes.

"Arrrggg," burst from the creature before he froze, unmoving.

"What?" Gage shook his badge, then went to shake the leprechaun...who stretched out his head on his neck and would have bitten Gage's hand if he didn't have such good reflexes and whipped it away in time.

"I'll turn *your* ass to stone, you pox bottle," the creature roared.

Daire pulled back Gage a few steps, for safety. "Look, maybe we find out his name, to command him," he suggested.

"Aren't they called things like Twinkle or Thistledown?" Gage replied.

"That's more fairies. Leprechauns are things like Lucky, or Jiggy," Daire mused.

The leprechaun glared murderously at them from his lumpy potato face.

"That sounds old-fashioned. I'm sure I heard that they have longer names now, like Birthday O'Malley or Cheery McMurphy," Gage suggested.

"I'll beat you shitehawks flat and stamp on your empty husks with your Birthdays or your Cheeries," was the answer to that.

"Maybe…Angry O'Connell," Daire couldn't resist saying.

"Eat my shite," yelled their prisoner.

"Or Sweary McClary." Gage snorted.

"So, you want to know my name, do ya? Here's my name." The leprechaun clenched his hand.

"Fisty?" Daire blinked.

"Knuckles. Knuckles O'Sandwich," the leprechaun corrected, his fists ready.

"You made that up," Daire accused.

"Only the surname. Test me," Knuckles invited.

"We're not here for a fight. We don't have time for a fight. We want a guide for safe passage over the rainbow." Daire had had enough of this.

"Guessed that, ballsac. Well, let's talk price?" Knuckles asked. He pulled against his bonds.

"Okay. Well, better untie him —" Daire instructed Gage, who loosened the ropes.

As soon as he had enough leeway to wriggle free, Knuckles yelled, "Hadaway and shite, losers," and ran for it.

" —but don't take your eyes off him," Daire finished.

Gage made the rope into a lasso and threw it, catching Knuckles easily. He pulled him back and tied Knuckles' wrist to his.

"Can't blame a chaun for trying." Knuckles shrugged. "A chaun's gonna chaun."

"What's this price?" Daire demanded.

"Well, see now, that depends." Knuckles dusted his clothes down then took a handkerchief from his pocket and rubbed it over his pate. "We set our own tariffs."

"Strong union." Gage approved.

"So we can ask for *anything*." Knuckles ignored Gage and looked at Daire.

"What do you want?" Daire had a bad feeling about this.

"Well..." Knuckles ground a toe into the dust and looked down coyly, then peeped up at Daire...who really hoped this wasn't going to involve Knuckles' shillelagh...or his lucky charms...

Chapter Thirteen

"A *date*. A gods-be-slapped *date*!"

Gage, on guard outside the changing room while Daire used it, was forced to listen to him complaining bitterly as he had every second since they'd left Knuckles.

"He couldn't have asked for a tooth or a finger? Something I would have given him more easily?" Daire raged next, above the swishes and whisks of the clothes he was trying on. "Or us to take him to the dentist!"

"You heard him." Gage ducked and just managed to catch the rejected clothes Daire expelled from the changing room by flinging them over the top of the curtain. The short curtain, whose gaps below and above were the reasons Gage was on guard there. No one should peep at Daire. "Heard what he said, that he hasn't had a date for three decades."

"I refer you to the dentist remark," Daire snapped.

Gage flinched at the wail from behind the door. "Those parachute pants no good?" he asked.

"They make my ass look fat!" Daire shrieked.

This small store, Vyntyge Pyxye, on the edge of town not far from the hinterland, had a very odd selection of clothes, but Daire had been reluctant to go farther into the capital, and they were time-crunched. Gage thought about what Knuckles had said, and about how and why leprechauns lived in the hinterland.

"I didn't realize chauns can't go into certain places, that they need to be accompanied by a pixie," he said.

"I'd never thought about it. And we think pixies have it rough," Daire replied.

Gage mused a little on segregation...and interspecies relationships. Griffins were thought to be elitist, keeping to their own kind, and he'd never seen a cross-species match, but he was here *because* of a relationship between two people from different species.

Catching a glimpse of Daire's mostly naked body when the curtain wafted up had him hardening in his pants. Griffins had flings outside their own race, and a fling was all this was, wasn't it? And it shouldn't even be that. He was here to work, not play, and yet, the more he thought about it, Daire going — no matter how reluctantly — on a date with another guy sat like a stone on his chest.

Well, he'd be there. With the number of enemies after him, Daire needed a bodyguard, even if Gage had made a lousy one so far. Having lost their subject to kidnappers was a pretty good sign he was shit at his job. Maybe he'd be a better chaperone, and he certainly intended to try, because he had no intention of Knuckles even holding Daire's hand, never mind stealing a kiss from him. He rubbed his stomach where it ached again. The curtain rattled back on its rail, Daire stomped out...and Gage's jaw dropped.

"Are those...leather pants?" he managed to ask. *Tight black leather pants. And knee-high black leather boots. And a long black leather coat.* "And that shirt..." That frilly white shirt that didn't have buttons but that was laced at the front. But not with lace. So why did they call it lace...when it was a leather thong, and not pulled tight but left loose so the shirt gaped open?

"And you're wearing eye makeup? And..." Lost for words, Gage pointed at Daire's hair, now a beyond-sexy tangle of waves and curls.

"Just a charm I'm trying," Daire muttered in reply. "A date's a date. Look, I haven't been out in ages, all right?"

"I'll take you out!" Gage shouted. He lowered his voice. "Dinner, a show...do you have theater here?"

"We...do," Daire answered softly, his gaze fixed on Gage, just as Gage's was on him. All he could see was this green-eyed, snub-nosed pixie with his beguiling ways, his tricksy spirit and his rebel heart. And those pointed pixie ears... Gage gulped. He wanted to fondle the tips, to lick them, to see if it was true what they said about them.

"Ahem?" An assistant had slid up to them and now fake-coughed.

"Chit it?" Daire asked Gage.

"Sirs!" the assistant looked from Daire to Gage.

"I mean can you get this on expenses?" Daire turned to the employee. "It's part of a Griffin Guardians assignment."

"I never had one that called for leather pants and eyeliner before," Gage replied.

Daire winked. "You never met me before."

True. He'd never met *anyone* like Daire before. Gage took a look around at the bright colors in this retro clothing boutique, relearning purple and red and turquoise, and picking out more everyday shades of brown and green in the outfits of pixies in the streets Daire hurried him through once they left. He'd never met anyone who was pursued by a terror-dactyl before either — Daire flattened himself against a wall when this one swooped low.

"Just in case," he joked.

It wasn't funny, though. It was how Daire lived — on the edge, his actions and antics risky. And Griffin Guardians...didn't. "Come on. We'd better hurry," he said. They really had to. They only had until the evening. They rushed through the streets to the place Knuckles had chosen.

"I never had an assignment that called for this before, either." Gage stared at the place. "*Minigolf?*"

"Or as Knuckles probably calls it, 'golf'. He must feel like a giant here. Think that's why he wanted to come?" Daire commented, his hand over his mouth to hide his laughter.

No, because he's never had the chance before, Gage thought, seeing the expression on the leprechaun's face as he gawked at everything. He looked...a lot less angry.

"Earth Minigolf." Gage read the sign on the entrance gate.

"This is what the human realm looks like," Knuckles insisted, as if Gage had said it didn't. "Every street in every town has a castle, there's lots of windmills everywhere, and those big sand triangle things, and towers, and statues..."

"Including one you have to hit the ball through to start?" Daire pointed at it. He took the club from Gage, who'd paid for two tickets. He looked up at Gage when

Gage nudged him and indicated the leprechaun, who stood waiting. "Oh, erm, yes, you look...nice, Knuckles?" he finished, handing him the club.

"Thanks." Knuckles fingered the two long thick bunches that his beard was now divided into. His beard seemed to start just above his ears, and was weird to see, when he had no hair on his head. Couldn't he sweep some over, or cut some off and make it into a toupee, Gage wondered? The way Knuckles glared at him suggested a lot of people thought and even said that. Gage took a step back and folded his arms, peering from left to right, narrow-eyed, like a bodyguard-chaperone did. Probably.

"You okay?" Daire gave him a glance, but his attention was on hitting the small white ball up the ramp to the Statue of Freedom's robes, with their hole. Their...strategically placed hole. "Score!" Daire punched the air at having hit his ball through the statue and out the other side. With a *bing bing bing* her torch lit up. "See that? I hit it just right!" he boasted.

"Nah. You hit her sweet spot, her crown spins," Knuckles told him. "My friend Clubfoot saw it."

"Do all leprechauns have descriptive names?" Gage asked. Knuckles nodded. "Then I'm sorry your friend has such a problem."

"Ain't no problem—little bastard enjoys clubbing feet," Knuckles answered. "Look."

They looked at the small, ferret-faced, ebony-haired leprechaun running up and striking a group of people on the foot before running away laughing as they hopped and cursed.

"Well, I say friend," Knuckles continued. "He's more like a father to me. Taught me everything I know."

Gage and Daire moved off a little and angled their feet away from Knuckles.

Gage thanked the sun, stars and moon that the golf course wasn't that extensive. He tried to decide on the worst hole. Maybe that poor statue lady, with her torch and book? Or the massive lion called a sfinxe, where the ball went in its mouth and out its back hole, its tail rising to reveal the exit? No, he really didn't like the next one, the pyramid where a bandage-trailing mummy rose and roared at whoever had disturbed his slumber.

"Remind me that if I ever go through the Veil, not to visit that desert kingdom. Eeejit, did they say it was called?" he asked Knuckles.

Daire wasn't listening. He was trying to hurry things along. "Well, if that's everything..." he said brightly to Knuckles.

Gage didn't like the way Knuckles was looking down at the tip of his toe that he was grinding into the ground. He liked even less how Knuckles looked up...and at the diner attached to the golf course.

"Seeing as we're all dressed up," he said, his gruff voice shy.

"Oh gods," Daire exclaimed, on seeing inside the diner, with its brightly colored ice creams, a knickerpixieglory the biggest of them.

"What is this music?" Gage wanted to grab napkins to stuff into his ears. "And that group playing it?"

"The Pixie League." Knuckles seemed to know all about it. "They're really good. Nearly as good as Pixie Ballet, and even better than Pixies go to Pixies Lands."

"I take back everything I thought about the minigolf. It was fine, in comparison," Daire muttered, his mouth falling open when Knuckles clambered up onto the small stage to sing along with the group.

"Is that…something that happens here, or is…?"

"It's just him," Daire answered Gage's trailed-off question.

Gage agreed, if the bewildered looks on the group's face were any indication. "He'll get hungry soon and come down," he reasoned. "That won't be as bad."

It wasn't. Knuckles eating a banana split was worse.

"I guess…chauns don't use spoons?" Daire said, as unable to tear his eyes away as Gage was. Although they both did when Knuckles used the end of his beard to mop up the last melted smears of ice cream from the bowl then sucked his strawberry-flavored hair with a smack of his lips.

That was disgusting, but Gage saw a lot of possibilities in cream, both ice cream and, gods-in-the-sky, *whipped*. But not here. Somewhere more romantic, which wouldn't be difficult to find. A meadow, where he and Daire were picnicking in the long clover-flowers, beside a stream. And where the heat made them strip off, and bathe in the fresh water, and come out, to let the sun dry them.

Well, for as long as Gage could keep his hands off Daire's naked body before throwing him onto his back, to drip honey onto his chest and lick it off, swirling his tongue around Daire's nipples, getting them puffy and reddened. Then he'd take up the whipped cream, but wouldn't anoint Daire's body with that, even though Daire would be wriggling with impatience and jacking his own cock, while Gage watched, encouraging him. He'd probably be stroking himself, his hard-on almost painful by then.

And when Daire was almost at the edge, Gage would squirt the whipped cream into his own mouth...before bending low to take Daire down to the root, the silky cream making the blowjob easier and making Daire harder, until he came, Gage swallowing two sorts of cream at once. He moved uncomfortably in his seat. He'd blown Daire just a short while ago, and come hard himself, thanks to Daire's clever tongue and lips, but he was growing hard again.

"Ah. That was good." Knuckles sighed.

Gage jumped. Leprechauns couldn't see into thoughts, could they? No, Knuckles was standing, and checking for any missed dessert on the floor, so he must be referring to that.

"Good date?" Daire asked, following Knuckles out, Gage trailing them.

"The best I ever had." Knuckles looked shy again. "The other was shite. I got stabbed in the throat."

There was no answer to that, Gage thought. Daire was speechless too.

"Right. Come on." Knuckles nodded.

"Where to now?" Gage asked, wary.

"Over the rainbow o'course, shite for brains." Knuckles grabbed their hands.

Chapter Fourteen

"And we really need all this?" Daire asked, in the aisle of Pix's Sporting Goods where Gage had insisted they detour to first. Well, he'd requested a place where he could get specialist equipment, and after the misunderstanding that had taken them into the combined koffi shop and adult entertainment store, Grind and Grind, they'd come here. It seemed to be more what he wanted. Daire, however, was bored.

"If we'll need it all? We won't know until we know. Be prepared and then some," Gage answered, hefting an ax and rejecting it for a bigger one.

"Is that the corps' new motto?" Daire couldn't resist teasing the griffin.

"No and you know it." Gage shook a finger at him then resumed eyeing up the shelf full of waterskins. "What's the pixie Guild motto? 'Go, Pixies, but not too far and expend the least amount of energy and effort as you do so'?"

"As if. That's much too long. No, it's just a shrug symbol." Daire gave a one-shouldered shrug in illustration.

"And you really need to do all this?" was his next question a little later, when they were back in the hinterland and Gage, now wearing the new outdoorsy clothes he'd acquired at the store, was busy again.

Gage answered with a simple nod *yes*.

Daire sat on the grass to think. On the one hand, watching Gage chop a log into firewood that he stowed in his pack, and lean into a fountain to fill waterskins that he tied *onto* his pack was a treat. Watching the strong, muscular griffin do most things was. "This get you going? Are you *erect...ing*...the tent?" Daire asked, loading his question with all the innuendo it would hold.

"Yes. Then I'm going to dismantle it," Gage replied. "Well, I might wet it first. So if either of you wants to wait inside, see how much — if any — water seeps in? It says it's waterproof but..." He subsided into muttering as he tugged at poles and canvas.

And on the other hand, watching Gage remind onlookers, mostly Daire, by his actions that he was a responsible, capable, federal law enforcement officer, one who'd be high-tailing it — literally — out of the Pixies Lands as fast as his wings could fly him the second the assignment was over *wasn't* as much fun. And Gage was clearly determined to get his mission over with as soon as possible. He needed to get back to his real life, which wasn't here, stuck with Daire the pixie.

Was there a place for Daire, in Gage's real life? Or could they have some kind of long-distance relationship? Daire snorted at the very thought. *The captain and the ne'er-do-well.* Daire wouldn't buy *that* story-parchment, even if it was free. *The griffin and the trickster pixie, who's a bad influence on the griffin.* Fuck long-distance. If Daire lov—was a friend to Gage, he should *keep* his distance, not get him into any more trouble.

Daire tore himself away and went to join Knuckles, who was leaning on a low branch and humming one of the songs the pixie group had played, something about Club Pixiecana where drinks were free, Daire thought. It sounded a good enough place to him.

"You can really ask for anything as a fee to guide people over the rainbow?" he asked.

"Yeah, anything. From the filthy rich who like it there and the just filthy who have business there." Knuckles spat on the ground. "Takes all sorts, don' it?"

"Oh. But mostly criminals, right?"

Knuckles nodded. "It's good for networking. Get what or who ya need, ya know?"

He sounded so professional that it startled Daire. "What if you don't feel like taking the job or don't like the look of the client?" he asked.

"Ah, ya just ask 'em for something impossible to get." Knuckles pulled a pipe with a really long stem from his pocket and sucked on the end.

Was it lit? Daire didn't think so. If it was, he feared for Knuckles' pockets, if nothing else. "Impossible? Like a left-handed screwdriver or rubber nails or a bucket of steam?"

"Yeah. Or something they can't or won't want to do." Knuckles jerked around at a noise coming up behind them. "Like this…"

"I beg your pardon?" The elf gaped at the leprechaun he was holding tightly, who was smirking fit to bust. "I must have misheard. I thought you said you wanted me to – "

"Kiss a troll's ass and get a picture of yourself doing it," the leprechaun said. "Clubfoot here'll make yer picture."

The black-bearded chaun stood ready with a sketchpad and pencil...and a wooden club.

"But I can't do *that!*" the elf burst out.

"No, you can't. Because the fee just went up. Now it's *French* kiss a troll's ass," the leprechaun said, miming obscene licking and slurping.

Daire gulped, realizing he'd gotten off lightly. He turned his attention back to Gage. He still couldn't believe how easy and right things felt between them, considering they were two very different species. It was almost unheard of, surely? Interspecies relationship... Something about that and the rarity started to wave across his mind, but the sight of Gage doing stretches then push-ups, then one-armed push-ups slammed it away.

He wondered what Gage was doing when he climbed a tree and looked far into the distance, squinting and nodding. When he came down, he made notes in a small pocket notebook, and even did a drawing.

"Knuckles?" Gage came over. "Would you say this was a fair representation of the terrain? Yes, the map's a little rough, but... And I'm presuming we're trekking over those mountains, meaning we're dealing with those hills, valleys and rivers?"

"Presume, do yer? Presume all yer like." Knuckles laughed as if at a private joke. "But this mean you pair are ready at last, then?"

"Well, yes." Gage nodded and after a second, Daire did too, trying not to recall any whispers or rumors he'd heard about going over the rainbow.

Knuckles gave a piercing whistle and a wizened leprechaun. his beard around his feet, came lumbering up, trundling a wooden cart. A small fire burned in the middle of it, more coals than anything, and a fat round pot swung over it, suspended on cords. A metal ladle slid around in it.

The pot rocked alarmingly when the old chaun tried to hurry at Knuckles' second whistle and impatient gestures and irritated words and tripped over his beard. No, more like his beard was trying to trip him up, winding around one ankle then the other, then both, like bindweed. The old chaun paused, to poke and jab at it then beat it back with his walking stick, then resumed his journey.

"Can't he just trim his beard?" Gage asked, then flinched from the daggers both leprechauns shot him from their eyes.

"Life's so easy for you, isn't it?" mocked Knuckles. "Trim this, cut this, squeeze this, rub this…"

Daire would have been more interested in pursuing that if the sound of thick liquid sloshing about inside the container hadn't captured his attention.

"Two?" the chaun asked Knuckles, reaching them.

Knuckles nodded. "Yeah, please."

The elderly carter ladled out two large splashes of whatever he pushed into two wooden beakers from a stack, and Daire and Gage each took one. Daire studied his. It was thick and golden, possessed of a dull shine. He went to put his finger in, to see the exact color, and perhaps taste it.

The strangled, alarmed noise from the carter stopped him.

"You don't wanna do that." Knuckles grinned, showing stumpy teeth. "But I thought you were in a rush?" He rolled his eyes at Daire and Gage's bewilderment. He mimed drinking then an arc shape with his other hand, making his fingers jump over it. "Then sup up yer drink and you'll be there."

"That's a pot of gold! Liquid gold!" Daire exclaimed, understanding, and confused at the same time. All the stories about leprechauns and gold and —

"Th-that's it?" Gage stammered. "No trekking, climbing, swimming, marching — we just *drink*?"

"Well ex-*cuse* me for not being a dryad and making you answer riddles or being a giant and making you perform feats of strength!" Knuckles spat back.

"But..." Gage stared into his cup.

"Quick as you can. Best if you can do it in one." Knuckles shared an evil smile with the carter.

"But —" Gage started again.

"Oh, just drink!" Daire couldn't take another second of Gage butting like a goat. To encourage him, he took as big as mouthful as he could of his cup...and nearly vomited. *Hells on a stick!* And he thought the yeast wheat beer with clove at the Neck was rough. Oh wait, it was. But this... The roughness didn't last...but turned worse.

"Oh my sacred secret stars!" Gage gagged. "It's burning! And now it's freezing. It's so bitter." He shuddered, his handsome face a little green. "And now it's salty."

"Oh, shut up with the commentary!" Knuckles moaned. "Yer think that's bad? Wait till you get to —"

"Dung." Daire held his nose at the evolution of the taste.

"Piss," Gage managed to get out.

Ogre snot. Troll sweat. Orc taint. Daire didn't know how he knew what each sip tasted of, but he did.

"Gets better." Knuckles nudged the carter, who nodded.

"Gets really better. Best taste ever," he agreed.

"'Ere." Knuckles took the elder chaun's stick from him and beat back his beard a little for him.

Gage. It tastes of Gage. Daire savored the mouthful, reliving the taste of kissing Gage, of his lips and tongue. The aftertaste was of the skin over Gage's sharp-cut, honed abs when he'd licked down them. Another sip brought him the remembrance of nosing into Gage's balls, to take one in his mouth and roll it on his tongue.

Gage stared at him, at the side of his neck where it met Daire's shoulder. He'd trailed his tongue down it and bitten it. Was that the best taste ever, for him? The connection between them, their ease and affinity with each other, stunned Daire anew. Was that how Gage felt too? That what was between them went beyond the physical? What did it mean?

"Nearly done?" Knuckles pushed between them. "Right. Drink it up together. Now!"

Startled by his shout, Daire drained the last of his leprechaun gold and what felt like the fastest, hardest pixie pouf ever happened. A slam, a bang—it was like running into a wall...then going through it.

"Rainbow!" Gage gasped.

"Don't talk. Oh, it don't do nothing, just I'm sick o' yer damn yapping," Knuckles told them.

Rainbow, yes. Inside the rainbow. Not going over the rainbow, but through. Daire experienced each color on his skin then inside his body. The heat of the red, the blaze of the orange, the warmth of the yellow, the brash spring hope of the green, the coolness of the blue and the pokes to his body and inside his mind of the indigo and violet. That and the sensation of traveling through water, air, light and earth turned him inside out.

With a whoosh, he dropped onto sand, Gage by his side. They landed on their feet, but Daire staggered, thinking he was going to throw up.

"Take a deep breath," Knuckles said, and Daire did. Gage too.

"Is it Monday?" Daire asked.

"Why?" Gage asked, straightening up and looking unfairly none the worse for wear, whereas Daire regretted his choice of leather pants. Okay, maybe not—they did amazing things for his ass and legs. "Monday, why?"

He looked alarmed. They'd have missed the deadline. "I feel dizzy and nauseated, like I do on Monday mornings." Daire mimed drinking too much.

"Ain't, no. Ain't no days or time here. It stands still," Knuckles said.

Daire did a double-take on looking at him—the leprechaun was big on this side of the rainbow. Taller than Daire. Knuckles just shrugged, his lips curling in a grin. "Perks of the job?" Daire guessed.

"Well. We'd better get searching for the Storm Queen." Gage brushed down his uniform. The sand they stood on was fine, flyaway. "She must be in some hellhole. Some spooky dungeon or scary castle or…"

Daire understood why he trailed off. He'd turned too, from the graceful curve of blond beach to the even prettier boulevard across from it. "Or in a luxury villa on a private estate," he finished for Gage, gaping at the high-end properties glowing soft creams and pinks and powder blues. "You can tell this place is expensive because of the smell."

The salt of the ocean was a soft tickle in his nose, the warm caramel color and aroma of the sand gently complementing it. Bushes of pink and red flowers lined the walkway, releasing fragrant bouquets into the air. It felt calm and peaceful.

Gage shielded his eyes and peered along the elegant bend of the road. "How will we know where she is?"

"You after a runaway?" Knuckles asked. "Yellow Palace."

"No..." Gage clearly didn't want to reveal too much.

"Someone got snatched? Nappees go into the third place along." Knuckles pointed.

"This realm is very organized," Daire commented.

Knuckles gave a shrug. "Well, this is where I see the back of yer."

"Oh." Daire hadn't thought of that, and his heart sank a little. He pulled Knuckles into a hug, and Gage enveloped him too the second Daire let him go. "Goodbye," he said. "We'll miss you. Take care, yes?"

"Ah, piss off ya losers!" Knuckles protested, turning away and rubbing at his eyes. "Damn sand gets everywhere." He sighed. "Look, seein' as we're gettin' all sentimental..." A knife appearing in his hand, he sawed an inch or two off his beard and handed it to Daire, then did it again for Gage. "You can braid it, make bracelets, or whatever, to wear. Whatever's fashionable where you are." He stood waiting. "Ahem?"

"Erm..." Daire was at a loss. "I don't know what..."

"Usual is a pinky, if yer don't wanna insult the whole race." Knuckles switched his small knife for a bigger one and advanced.

"*No!*" Gage protested, blocking him.

"Ha! Got yer good there!" Knuckles burst out. "Ah, chaun humor. Ain't nothing like it."

Daire was glad about that as, wiping tears of laughter this time from his eyes, Knuckles vanished.

Chapter Fifteen

"Did he feel your ass too when he hugged you?" Daire asked Gage.

Gage nodded. "Oh yeah. And stole coins from my pocket."

Gage knew they should move, but he couldn't stop looking at the beautiful long length of land stretching between the ocean and the distant mountains. The ocean... Gage had never seen it before, or such soft, fine sand. He let some fall between his fingers, appreciating the color and all the blues and greens of the water lapping it.

"I know." Daire inhaled the salt. "Wish we could just relax here, sun showering. Well, didn't Knuckles say time stands still here? We could —"

"We couldn't." Gage couldn't go along with that. "I'm just curious. Never been here before."

"Guardians have no jurisdiction here," Daire pointed out, leading Gage from the sands to the sidewalk. "It's a safe haven."

He seemed to approve. Gage had heard rumors of the outlaw realm, but had expected mean streets — well, okay, he'd imagined a forest — full of desperados, grifters, hitmen, thieves and pimps. Not this quiet, discreet paradise for rich people. He saw no signs of authority or law, so how was it monitored, or policed?

"Did that...? Did you see that?" Daire pointed with his elbow at a statue on a plinth. He covered his mouth with his hand and continued in a whisper, "I think that statue was facing the other way a second ago. It moved!"

He was right. Each statue they passed swiveled and turned, tracking their movement and answering Gage's question about monitoring. He jumped when a metal post with a light circle on its top bumped his head...by bending down to them as they walked by.

"You're the avian expert," Daire commented. "Do these birds look suspicious to you?"

"Not suspicious. Professional." Gage was familiar with using worker avians and although these weren't the papagae he was used to, he thought the matching blue and white birds had a similar function. Well, using an avian network was one way to keep an eye on things, and at least they were pretty.

The hedge they were walking along bore sweet-smelling pale pink flowers, and Daire picked one and inhaled its fragrance.

"Sort of coco-nuss scent," he said. He beckoned Gage to bend a little then tucked the bloom through his buttonhole.

"What's that for?" Gage asked. He was touched, but suspicious.

Daire grinned. "To see if that offer of a ride on your shoulders is still open. Have you seen how far we'll have to trek along this road? These properties are set in enormous grounds!"

"And those boots aren't comfortable?" Gage guessed. "You could always take them off."

"You'd like that. Any excuse to get me naked." Daire prodded him.

"What? It's not like I suggested taking your pants off!" Gage protested. "Although...them being black leather, you do look hot in them."

"Thank you."

Daire pretending to take his words as a compliment reminded Gage of how the pixie had behaved when they'd met. Which...had been just yesterday? *Gods.*

"We need transport," Daire complained, then looked around at a whirring noise.

A conveyance slid along the road and stopped next to them. It was somewhere between a cart and a carriage, small, compact, and...horseless. Daire looked at Gage and Gage looked back at him. Daire shrugged.

The horseless transport's door opened, and Gage saw it was also driverless. "Should we...? I mean, it seems it's for us?" he asked.

"Probably rude not to." Daire pushed past him and sat in the back. "Ahh. That's better. Third property along, please, Mr. Carriage. Gage, get in. I bet it's a courtesy service here. All arrivals must get it, whether they're just simply rich and have a second home here in this pretty place or..." He mouthed *criminal*.

"So it's like a hub." Gage recalled Knuckles' words that he'd caught. "A high-end version of a seedy tavern where you go to meet contacts you need for the kind of job you need done. *Ow.*" He rubbed the top of his head where it had hit the roof of the carriage when the vehicle sped up and thumped over a bump in the road.

It seemed the carriage was sensitive to criticism of its workplace.

"Try to blend in," Daire whispered. "You can't go throwing your feathers about here, remember. You're not here as a Guardian. You have to work undercover."

"What are we here as then?" Gage asked. He liked every detail of an assignment down in black and white and committed to memory.

"I'll figure it out as we go." Daire patted Gage's knee, his hand making Gage's skin warm, even through the thick fabric of his mountaineering clothes. "We could be fraudsters, intriguers, mercenaries…generally sleazy individuals evading the law. Let me think…"

Gage wasn't reassured.

The carriage turned into the well-maintained drive of a luxurious pastel-pink and baby-blue property, where uniformed doormen gave small bows and opened the wide doors for them. The same pale colors were used in the marble and glass atrium, and the few people idling about were well-dressed. A circular desk stood under a round skylight. The place, whatever it was, whispered *money*.

"May I help you?" asked a woman Gage thought might be human. The touches of lemon yellow on her uniform matched those of the men at the door. "Sirs?" she prompted.

Now was the time for Daire, who'd been figuring it out, to speak up, but he was too busy gawking all around him to answer.

"Have you booked?" the woman asked.

Oh, was this place a hotel? That made sense! "No," Gage admitted. He tried to make a rough estimate of what a stay in such a classy place would cost and arrived at *above my pay grade. Now and forever.* He looped an arm around Daire to keep him close and not let him wander off and get into trouble that they'd have to buy their way out of. No way would the Guardians honor that chit when it came due, apart from the fact that a corps captain shouldn't be here.

"We're not here for that," he continued to the assistant.

"Oh, of *course.*" The woman looked from him to Daire, looked Daire up and down, then back to Gage again. "You came up and in the main entrance, didn't you?"

Gage replied with a gesture that could have been a nod or a head shake. He wasn't going to commit himself.

The receptionist bent across her circular marble counter to them. "I know what you're here for," she whispered. "You came in the wrong section. It's happened before. Guests are eager, but nervous." Her smile looked designed to comfort those eager, nervous, section-mistaking guests.

Gage made the same head-wobble gesture again.

"You want the Dungeon," she continued, her voice low.

"Dungeon!" Daire echoed, nudging Gage.

Yes, dungeon, *where kidnap victims are probably held.* Gage got it.

"I'll get a member of staff to walk you around to where you want to go." She straightened up and dinged a bell, the sound musical in the large atrium.

Well, this was easier than Gage had expected. Things *were* very organized.

"I bet with this realm being the way it is, people here to rescue the nappee probably meet with the nappers under very civilized conditions," Daire guessed. "There's maybe a mediator or middle person?"

"Could be. Let's get there quickly and bring this to a close." Gage prepared to hustle.

"Sirs, you do know magic is not permitted on the premises?" the receptionist said. "So I'm afraid I'll just have to check if you're bearing any. Should that be the case, it will be removed, placed in safe keeping and returned to you when you exit the premises."

She dinged the bell twice and, with a slight buzzing whir, a tiny elemental creature peeled itself from the glass skylight above. Gage wouldn't have seen it even if he'd been searching, because it was transparent, looking like a figurine made of crystal or frozen water. It dipped lower, to whirl around Gage, who resisted the temptation to swat at it, or scratch the slight itch he felt—inside his head.

It turned grass green, then pulled away, hovering in the air until it returned to its original translucent state. The assistant smiled her thanks at Gage. He'd barely understood what had happened when the elemental whisked around Daire and turned from grass to pea to orc-green within a heartbeat.

"Oh, I see you divested yourself well prior to arrival. Good idea to give yourself time to get used to it, hm?" The receptionist gave Daire a smile too.

"But... I—" Daire had turned almost as green as the creature had. "I have no magic?" he whispered.

"It's fine," Gage reassured him. Maybe pixies were sensitive about it. Like orcs were about the size of their—

"Oh, it's *really* not."

Gage couldn't understand the expression on Daire's face. His color was draining, leaving him paler than he had been. Wait…color. Gage whipped his head around, assuring himself he could see the lemon yellow of the place's corporate livery, and the pretty pinks and blues of its décor. He'd seen the honey brown of the sand too. And yet Daire had no magic about him. So how could Gage be seeing colors? What did that make him think of — some griffin myth or story —

"Ah. Here he is. Pleasure to assist you." The receptionist's final smile was one of dismissal.

Gage lost his train of thought as he tracked the progress of the staff member making its way toward them. "It's a kura-kura," he said a little redundantly, of the large, low and long-necked reptile, its hard shell painted the hotel's yellow, still making its way to them. Its *slow* way to them.

"Good thing time stands still here," Daire muttered.

They followed the animal through the atrium and had run out of polite conversation to make by the time they'd reached a side corridor. The kura nodded his agreement to their "*lovely place*" and "*nice décor*" slowly and shook his head to their "*is it far?*" even more slowly.

"Here?" Gage looked at Daire when they stopped in front of a door. "Well, thanks."

The kura didn't move. It would be rude to reach and step over him, wouldn't it?

"I think he wants a tip," Daire whispered.

"Oh…" Gage patted his pockets. He had things to survive in the wild with, but something a hard-shelled reptile would eat? His fingers landed on the blossom Daire had picked for him and the kura's beady eyes brightened. "Really? Here." He bent to offer it, sad to see it go, and jumped back at the snap of the kura's jaws grabbing for the bloom. Munching, the reptile ambled off.

"Here goes..." Gage pushed open the door, steeling himself for— A spa? A health club? Some place with lots of soft green climbing and trailing plants, the tinkle of water and the waft of nose-pleasing herbal scents.

"Sign in, please!" called a receptionist who could have been twins with the one they'd just left.

"Give a fake name!" Daire reminded him, and Gage's mind went blank. He cast around for any other name than his.

"Commander Slate? Really?" Daire griped, from where he stood next to him filling in his own form.

"Yes, Adam the Dwarf." Gage rolled his eyes.

"And that's your real age?" Daire sniggered. "I didn't know that. You don't look a day over sixty."

"And what did you put under allergies—work?" Gage tried to see.

"It's not an allergy. More a sensitivity. It's a species thing. You wouldn't understand." Daire huffed.

"Fine...fine..." The receptionist cast a glance over their forms. "And the payment... Fine, fine." She took the entire pouch before Gage could tip out any coins. "Go on through!"

"Well, I like how calm and civilized this is," Gage remarked. He pushed at the far door into what waited beyond. "It's all—"

"Black. With flashing lights and pounding music," Daire finished for him, shoving him inside whatever the room beyond was when he stood stock-still.

"But this isn't a dungeon!" Gage protested. One look around told him that.

"No, it's *the* Dungeon!" replied a staff member popping up...in an outfit that made Gage's assless pants look like parade uniform. "Let's get you through to the preparation and waiting rooms, shall we? Dom or sub?"

He addressed this to Gage, who tried to answer, only he'd forgotten words. And how to make his mouth muscles work.

"Dom or sub?" the assistant asked, louder. "Dom? Sub?"

"Sub?" Gage started to ask what the employee meant, and the assistant nodded.

"Well, yes." The guy smiled knowingly. "With tonight being the night it is! But we always check," he said. "Now, prep...A, B or C?" This was to Daire.

"Prep?" Daire looked lost. "Well, see — "

"Uh-huh." The assistant winked. "Come along then. Let's take you through."

"Daire?" Gage asked. He took another glance around at what the people were wearing — or not wearing — and caught the distant sound of whips and chains. Those things, added to the moans that were more pleasure-drenched than pain-wracked — although there was some of that in the mix — gave him a lot of clues as to what the Dungeon was. Who it catered for. And gods in a cave, he was...intrigued.

"We-we should stay, to see what we can find out, right?" Daire asked, his pupils huge as he looked at Gage. He licked his lips.

Gage nodded, his dick stiffening. "We...should."

He didn't think they'd learn any information useful for the assignment, but he was eager to see what the place had to show him...

Chapter Sixteen

The barely dressed assistant led Gage away. "You'll see your boy soon!" he trilled to Daire.

"Gage?" Daire called, recalling a second too late he should have said *Slate*, the fake name Gage had signed in under.

Gage slowed and looked at Daire over his shoulder. Daire studied his face carefully. He'd seen Gage alarmed, reluctant and even disgusted in their short time so far, and if he caught even a speck of those feelings. he was calling a halt to this now.

Sure, Gage had been curious and even eager a minute ago, but when push came to plug, as the saying went, it might be a different story. Daire wouldn't let Gage go through with anything like this if he wasn't one hundred percent into it. He'd pretend it was he himself who wanted to bow out, if Gage needed to save face. Daire could take that.

I...will? I can? The strength of his connection to and the nature of his feelings toward the griffin swept over him in a wave that was much stronger than the polite little rolls of ocean water he'd watched from the beach earlier. *This* wave rocked him on his feet. Daire put his feelings together with the way he and Gage...*fitted*, was the best he could come up with.

He wasn't a poet, declaiming on a stage in a tavern like Brackish did when it was buy one goblet, get one half off at the Neck. Nor was he a traveling player, spouting nonsense in rhyme from the back of a pageant wagon.

As much as he was trying not to think about it, the fact that he was able to work magic around Gage was there, front and center in his head. The suspicion that he was tapping into Gage's strength and power in some way solidified into a certainty, especially when he thought about how Gage got twinges to his stomach whenever Daire did it. The reason he was trying to deny the very idea was because the only way he'd ever heard about that happening meant that what he and Gage shared was more than a connection — they shared a bond.

"Gage?" he asked again, doubting Gage could hear him above the music and chatter. He went to form a question but stopped. Curiosity and longing shone from Gage's face...and he was as hard as a rock. "See you in a minute." Daire grinned. Whatever was going on, whatever mission he and Gage were on, this was what they were doing now.

"This way." Another employee led Daire forward a few feet to a small wooden bar counter, as Gage went through another door.

"Are the drinks included?" Daire asked automatically.

"Indeed!" The assistant beckoned the bartender over. "Non-alcoholic, of course."

"I know." The guy standing next to him interpreted the droop to Daire's mouth. "Drink as much as you like for free...as long as there's no alcohol in it. But it's a strict rule here in the Dungeon, and it's for the best."

"And the non-alc spelt-wheat ale isn't too bad," the guy on the other side of the first speaker said.

"I'm trying the non-grain wiski." The first one raised his glass.

Daire tried to work out what they were. Some kinds of fairies? Or was the second one a hob, or a goblin? He wasn't clear on the difference, or even if there was one. They were both about his height, and glancing around showed him that none of the males here were tall or bulky. He couldn't see any bigger beings or species.

"Virgin?" the fairy with the wiski asked him.

Daire raised a brow. "You talking about me or the drink?"

The fairy chortled. "I'd say you were experienced. First time here?" he clarified. "I'd have remembered all that lovely leather. Leather for pleasure, I say."

"Looks like a uniform, almost," the fake-spelt-wheat ale drinker said. "Oh, and talking of looking..."

Panels were being lifted in a wall close by. It wasn't a solid wall, but more like a partition, one they could see through, to the bays beyond.

"Come on!" The wiski fairy beckoned Daire over. Most of those present huddled around.

"But what's...go...ing..." Daire didn't need to finish his sentence. Not when he could see what was going on, on the other side of the screens. In a weird way, it reminded him of fathers pressed against the glass to watch their newborn pixlings in the incu-pods of the birthing hospital, or so Clove had described it to him. He'd been there to see the pixling he'd had with

Alletta...and the one he'd had with Elfie. At the same time. As the ladies had discovered when Clove had turned up.

Clove still had marks from the face-pox they'd paid a black sorcerer to visit upon him, their vengeance when they'd pieced things together and compared dates and times. As Trannell told him, they were lucky they enacted their revenge on that part of his body, and not lower. And it proved the depth of their feelings for Clove, Trannell had gone on to argue — flaccidity charms were a lot cheaper, easier to have cast...and lasted longer.

Only, there was nothing babylike or soft and sweet about what Daire was currently viewing. His jaw dropped at the sight of the big, tough — and naked, its hairy ass on display — troll...on all fours, being fitted with a saddle and bridle.

"But how — ?" Daire started to ask, only to find his question answered when a few taps with a riding crop got the protesting troll's mouth open enough to fit a metal bit in it, to which all the bridle pieces, including the reins, attached.

"I love how it keeps his mouth open." The voice somewhere near Daire's ear made him jump, and he turned to see a deva, a tiny fairy that looked almost like a firefly. "Keeps him at the ready, if you know what I mean." His wings quivering had him vibrating in the air as he rubbed his hands together.

Daire yanked his gaze away, and it landed on the giant in the stall next door. A giant who was strapped to a frame, pulling against his bonds and probably screaming, if his wide-open mouth and rolling-wide eyes were any indication. Daire had no need to ask why — the giant was reacting to the red-hot needle that gowned and masked assistants were bringing to his nipple...and piercing through it. The giant's scream was almost audible now when the assistant clamped a heavy-looking ring through his nub, and was clearly one of pleasure.

"Oh, it's not his first time. We do this every session. Their flesh heals itself," the wiski-drinking fairy explained to Daire, noticing his expression. "Still, means you get to do it again and again, right?"

"Right?" Daire echoed, watching the second needle approaching the giant...lower down his body. The giant's cock was so hard it was flushed an almost angry-looking purple shade. "Wait. You're having him pierced there? And there? And with those?"

Each assistant held up a silver bar that had a silver ball on each end.

"Gland and shaft? Yes." The fairy licked his lips. "It feels wonderful."

For who? Daire wondered. Well, to be fair, the giant seemed into having metal rammed through his cock, even though he was yowling, sweating and almost breaking his restraints.

"Put the speakers on!" the deva begged the fairy.

"Oh, all right." The fairy made a gesture to the monitor overseeing events on the other side of the glass, and sobs and whimpers flowed out.

"Please...*please*," begged the giant, struggling as one uniformed assistant lifted his cock, still massively erect after they'd pierced the shaft, and the other, needle in hand, reached for the head.

"He can be the scared whelp here. He can't anywhere else. He has to be tough and mean every day and everywhere else," the fairy explained, not even flinching at the blood-freezing scream his partner gave at the slide of the needle through his glans — or his eardrum-destroying moan when he spasmed in a massive, whole-body orgasm.

"Every time." The fairy chuckled, pride in every line of his face.

Daire knocked the back of his hand into the bottom of his chin to get his mouth to close.

"Oh, I know. Mine's the same." A glowing sprite nodded at the next space along, where a huge, mean-looking ogre in a short white paper gown was lying on his back on an examination table, cringing and shrinking into himself as straps were fastened across his chest and stomach...and his legs bent at the knees and his feet secured in stirrups.

His — and most of the spectators' — gaze was pinned to a tray of gleaming metal instruments being carried over to him.

"Clamps and rectal speculum."

Which made Daire feel as faint as the ogre looked.

"Oh, yours is ready." The fake-spelt-wheat ale drinking goblin nudged Daire, who stumbled a few steps, coming to a halt outside Gage's room.

He didn't know what he'd see, but it was Gage, seemingly fresh from the shower, a towel around his hips and patting himself dry with a second. Oh, those stray droplets running along the hewn planes of his torso!

Daire held his breath as Gage was led to lie face-down on a table, but it was to have a shoulder and upper back massage.

"Getting him relaxed, before you get him worked up?" The goblin nudged Daire again. "Good one."

"And he's C. See and be seen!" joked the fairy.

Daire didn't understand that, but understood that Gage was relaxed, enjoying the masseur's long strokes across his muscles, but his head, which he had turned to one side on the pillow, shot up as an assistant came over, carrying a tray on which lay several tails. Tails on plugs, Daire saw. Differently sized plugs, some smaller, some medium-sized and some hugely bulbous.

Gage looked up from that and caught Daire's eye and the next thing Daire knew, although having difficulty walking with his huge hard-on, he was inside the small alcove, beckoned over by the assistant who pushed the glass aside and closed it after him.

"Option C?" he confirmed, when Daire's face must have shown the puzzlement he was feeling.

C...as in 'see and be seen'. Daire understood now. Understood that the spectators out there would be watching him, in here. His eyes on Gage, he nodded, and Gage nodded back. He was aroused too. The slutty little griffin! Oh, Daire was going to enjoy this. He signaled to Gage to lie down again, and whipped the towel from him, exposing him, more so when he widened his legs and pushed one up a little.

"Gods," Daire breathed, rubbing his thumb over Gage's pucker, peeking from between his toned ass cheeks. "You ever had a plug in this sweet hole before?" Much less a tail, sweeping the floor where he crawled on hands and knees... He wasn't surprised when Gage gave a tiny nod, but the whoosh of jealousy that flared through Daire on knowing that did surprise him.

The trust and anticipation in Gage's blue eyes had Daire's breath catching in his throat. He took the bottle from the stand next to the bed and tipped some lube onto his fingers, then stroked them down Gage's crease before rubbing them over his pucker, spreading the sharp-scented liquid. Gage's moan was Daire's reward.

Daire circled the tip of his forefinger around Gage's hole before pushing in. He loved the taut resistance of Gage's ass and rotated his finger, forcing in then pulling out, fucking Gage with his hand, listening to the little cries Gage gave at each thrust. Those, and Daire's heavy breathing, were the only sounds audible. If the spectators out there were making any noise, they couldn't be heard in here.

Gage had closed his eyes but opened them suddenly, and his gaze locked with Daire's as Daire pulled free of the heated clutch of Gage's ass and thrust in another finger. The way this had Gage clenching around him brought a groan to Daire's lips. "Let me try…" he began, giving up on words and showing Gage what he intended.

To twist and curve his fingers, feeling for the bump of Gage's first gland, then the smaller one of his second. Did griffins speak their own language? Because it seemed Daire could only understand a few words Gage was saying, such as *gods* and *yes* and *more*. Or maybe it was a command or compulsion, because it had Daire sliding his fingers free to use them to unbutton his pants then pull his dick out. Ideally, he'd have worked Gage a little more, making sure he was loose enough, but he couldn't.

All he could do was line his cock up with Gage's entrance and surge deep into his scalding heat, not stopping until his hips met Gage's ass. "Best feeling ever," he tried to explain, just as it was the best sight ever, his cock buried in Gage, then emerging when Daire withdrew. He pulled out and drove back in, the force of his stroke rocking Gage's body under him.

Gage mewled. There was no other word for the noise that emerged from his big strong griffin, and Daire fucking loved how he'd reduced the tough soldier to this. "You want to come?" he whispered, taking Gage's jerky head movement as a *yes* and *please* and *now*. He reached around to fist Gage's dick — Gage had leaked a puddle onto the table and almost worn a groove in it with his rutting.

"*Yesss*," Gage hissed.

Understanding — feeling the same — Daire pulled out and slammed back in, deeper and harder than he had, grazing over one, two...*three* glands inside Gage. Gage's entire body stiffened, and he roared, his ass squeezing Daire's cock. He pumped into Daire's hand just as Daire shot into Gage's channel, both of them crying out when their cocks jetted long streams.

"Holy gods!" Daire's knees gave way under the force of his release. He'd never come that hard. His head spun and his ears rang. He caught movement out of the corner of his eye and turned to see a line of spectators on the other side of the viewing screen, a lot with bulges in their pants and each and every one applauding.

Yeah. They should. We deserve that. Just as Gage deserves to have whatever he needs. Whatever he wants.

Realizing the depth of his feelings for Gage left Daire stunned.

Chapter Seventeen

Dizzy, Gage couldn't take his eyes from Daire, and jumped when one of the attendants came in. Or came over — they could have been there the entire time for all Gage knew, just as he'd been barely aware of the spectators beyond the viewing pane.

Although, having them there, knowing eyes watched him and Daire... His heart beat faster even now. Exhibitionism wasn't the sort of thing Griffin Guardians indulged in. They didn't indulge themselves in much, really. Not like pixies. *Not like Daire.*

"Of course," he replied to whatever the assistant had said. Oh, Daire was being shown out. Gage would rather he stayed. He liked being with him, doing things together with him. And not just sex, although *gods above and below*, the pixie could fuck. Gage *ached*. He'd thought it a myth about griffin shifters possibly having a third, smaller and hidden prostate. No one he knew had ever said they had one, that anyone had found it. Well, fine, it wasn't the sort of subject routinely brought up in conversation at the HQ.

"We'll bring him back in a moment," the assistant promised Daire, who seemed as reluctant to leave as Gage was to have him go.

Well, great sex created bonds. And that was what was between them, what they had. All they had. Because what more could there be? Yet still he tracked Daire's exit and wished he'd gone with him when he saw what the room attendants were bringing over to him...to fit on him.

"Don't say a word," he warned Daire when he was led out to him a short while later. "Not about the outfit, or — "

"The cock cage?" Daire's green eyes bulged from his head. He accepted the leather leash when the attendant passed it to him. "Because that's what it is, isn't it?"

"It is and I want it off," Gage got out through gritted teeth.

"I don't think we can, not right now," Daire replied. *If that tricky pixie's enjoying this —*

"We have to play a part, remember?"

Because Gage suspected he was enjoying this. "I don't like it!" he insisted.

"Well, just think yourself lucky I'm not making you crawl." Daire nodded at another tall, broad sub...on his hands and knees, trailing after his elven-looking master.

Oh yeah, he was *so* enjoying this. "Let's..." Gage took a breath. "Get on with the assignment, all right? Trying to find what information we can here? I didn't get a chance to speak to anyone other than the attendants, who were useless — did you?"

Daire shook his head. "Not really. We'd better explore. The place. Not...anything else. Although..." He tugged on the leash.

"Come on." Gage dragged in a breath. "So you think we'll find something in one of these rooms? Maybe this first one? This Lightning Room?"

Lightning as in lightning *fairies*, he learned. A whole host of lightning fairies, gathered into a bright white ball that darted over the stretched-out body of a sub, zapping bolts through it. The sub writhed and arched, shrieking when the hits landed, his dick rock-hard and leaking.

"Fairy-fucked." The sub's Dom sighed, swiping his thumb over the head of his sub's cock then licking it. "There's nothing like it."

It was obvious there was no group of kidnappers in that room, waiting to do business with those wanting the nappee back. Gage elbowed Daire. "Try a bigger room."

Daire led him along the main area. "This one?" he asked. "It's bigger."

Ah. Because it housed a cockatrice. Gage had rarely seen the legendary beast, a two-legged dragon with a rooster's head, before and never seen one that allowed itself to be ridden. Well, this one barely did, bucking and spinning when its — naked — rider was placed on its back.

"Shining stars and gleaming moons!" Daire covered his ears at the shrieks and screams. "What's making the riders react like that? All they're doing is getting bumped over its scales… Ah. I just answered my own question, didn't I?"

"I knew cockatrice scales were highly prized." Gage peered as hard at them as Daire was. "But I didn't know why." He did now — they aroused wherever they touched. The rider slipping to the floor just now was too horny to walk, humping the air.

"Highly prized, you say? How...highly?" Daire's fingers twitched.

"Don't even think about it," Gage warned. "You don't want to know what a cockatrice does if it feels someone plucking one out. Let's just say you'd find it difficult to get aroused ever again, with what he'd pluck out of you, in turn."

Daire winced. "Point taken. Or not taken. Ever, I hope. Come on. Let's try another room."

They did, and quickly backed out. "So that's why unicorns are so hunted, and especially by virgins!" Gage gulped. "I don't think I can ever unsee that." Hadn't he seen something like it earlier? Some of the toys at Grind and Grind seemed to have been modeled on the unicorn's...horn. He sighed. "It's clear what we're looking for isn't here. Let's search the rest of this place."

Checking they weren't observed, they slipped out through a small side door into a service corridor. "That's better." Gage wasn't a fan of loud music and flashing lights. "Get this thing off me now." He flicked the cock cage.

"Me? I have no idea how it goes on or off!" Daire exclaimed. "Don't you?"

"I'm a Griffin Guardian, trained in law enforcement—it might surprise you to hear this, but removing cock cages isn't really part of those duties!" Gage yelped.

"I meant, because it has a padlock?" Daire indicated it. He lifted Gage's dick to examine the contraption...and Gage howled.

"It's to stop me getting erect, so *don't* go groping me," he commanded.

"You wish. You wish you were so tall and muscular and had such a bubble butt I couldn't keep my hands off it!" Daire accused. "That you were so sexy, with those blue eyes, that blond hair and chiseled features that all I wanted to do was throw you down and eat you out!"

"Just like you wish you were so irresistible, with those gleaming green eyes and pert, turned-up nose and gods-in-the-sky pointed ears and that trim little body that all I wanted was to suck your cock!" Gage raged.

In the silence that fell after that, they just looked at each other. "So," Daire said eventually, "where's the key?"

"Ah." The attendant had said something about it, but Gage's head had been too fuzzy after his orgasm to take it in. It still felt fuzzy now.

"Never mind. Let me try something. Unlock," Daire demanded.

The padlock fell to the floor, the leather cage dropped off and Gage's dick sprang free.

"That's better," Gage sighed, then rubbed his stomach where it churned a little. *Wait. What — ?*

"Let's see what's in here." Daire's voice was flat as he pushed open the door to a closet. "Look, staff uniforms." He tried to pull the hotel pants and tunic over his clothes and there were tears in his eyes when it became apparent there was no way he could conceal his long leather coat and he had to leave it off.

Gage was glad to get out of what he...wasn't wearing, even if it meant donning the kind of suit the doormen had worn and that was on the short and tight side, especially over his corps uniform. Daire had gone quiet, and Gage wondered if it was the sight of him in these unflattering pants and tunic causing it. No, it wouldn't be. Oh gods, was he regretting what they'd just done?

If anyone should be, it should be me! As a Guardian, he should be focused on the assignment, not taking a detour into...that. *This whole thing with Daire is a detour.* But he was enjoying the side trip and the partner he was making it with. *Partner.* He stumbled on the word. The concept. He'd never had one, outside his Guardian duties. He hadn't had much, outside his Guardian duties. And he couldn't really have this, could he? Whatever *this* was.

It was something that had made him want to do things with Daire he'd never done with anyone else. Never even thought of doing. But the exploration, the give and take, all seemed so natural, so much a part of his feelings.

Feelings.

He glanced at Daire in the gloom of the corridor. A beam of light from some small window above fell across him, showing the green of his eyes and the red of his lips. The colors...and Daire had no magic about him. Hadn't for a while, the receptionist had said.

"Daire." He hadn't known he was going to speak until he did, but there were things he had to ask. To know.

"Gage." Daire's tone matched his, but not in a mocking way. "I know. We...have to talk." He looked furious about it. "But not here. Not now."

Well, yes, the back corridor in what was possibly the enemy stronghold wasn't the best place for a griffin-pixie heart-to-heart.

"When this is over," Daire said, still looking angry.

Gage nodded. His hand brushed Daire's, and Daire clasped it, twining his fingers with Gage's, who instinctively tightened his around Daire's. Such a simple act, but Gage's heart stuttered a little at it. A crooked little laugh escaped from him. "I've never held hands while on an assignment before," he commented.

"Assignment," Daire repeated. "Mission." That was what this was. He'd been given this ability to siphon off Gage's griffin power in his role as assistant for the task they were charged with, because this job called for different skills than Gage had. His species didn't have the affinity with magic that this case called for, so the powers that be had...seen that and made provisions and...

Daire shook his head. For a pixie who prided himself on his lying and invention, he wasn't even fooling himself. Pixies didn't really bond nowadays. They found partners, yes, but once upon a time, or so old stories said, pixies had bonded heart, mind and soul with their mates. The ancient words, about the union of all three elements that made up a person, were still part of the handfasting ritual, for those who bothered with such ceremonies. That was mainly the rich, using it as an occasion to show off.

Daire was part of Gage's soul, now. Being able to access his strength and power was proof. Would they be able to see into each other's minds at some point, like old legends said? But that would mean he was in Gage's heart. Had Gage fallen for him? If he had, did he know? Griffins weren't traditionally given to self-reflection.

Well, Daire wasn't gonna be the sappy pixie, pining for the impervious big bold griffin shifter or, even worse, the indifferent big bold griffin shifter. As if there could be anything more than some convenient quickies on their shared mission! That made sense. *Soul, heart and mind indeed.* No, just convenient…soul-shaking, heart-stopping, mind-melting sex they indulged in every chance they got. Every chance they made.

"Grrr!" Daire stamped a foot. "Are griffins honest, as a species?"

"Oh yes." Gage straightened and stood tall. Well, as tall as he could without splitting his too-small uniform. "We're known for it."

"Typical." Daire stamped his other foot. "Typical!"

Gage dropped his hand, and that left Daire's empty and cold. Daire didn't like it, so he took it back again and for some reason brought it to his lips and kissed the back. "I *like* you," he ground out.

Gage looked down at him, his blue eyes bright. "I like *you*," he replied, sounding puzzled by that as much as by the conversation they were not having.

"Good!" Daire snapped.

"Good?" Gage sounded confused.

"Yes!" Daire snapped, louder. "Come on. That door there leads back into the hotel section, and I can get it open. Just don't…talk about how. Or anything, really."

He focused on accessing Gage's strength as softly as he could, gently, easily, and this time Gage didn't react. No rubbing of his stomach, no bewildered look or turn of his head as though he sensed something but couldn't figure out what it was.

The corridor beyond the easily opened door led to the hotel, and they hurried to read the signage there.

"Holding Suites! Look, that arrow's pointing to them!" Gage exclaimed. "This must be where the kidnap victims are kept!"

"They probably call them subjects or even guests," Daire replied. "Not victims. Yeah, dank cellars or high towers wouldn't really fit here, would they? Right, let's go do the rescue thing."

And get the assignment over.

And with it, him and Gage.

Chapter Eighteen

"Go carefully," Gage whispered. They were walking along a more brightly lit and more frequently used corridor. "There might be surveillance." He tried to harness the Guardian training and experience he usually had at his fingertips. It wasn't even second nature — it was so ingrained, so much a part of him that he would have classed it as his actual nature.

"We should be doing something," he said. He tried to recall how to blend in, when he was on an assignment. Daire's proximity made it difficult to think. Reluctantly he stepped away a little.

"We are doing something." Daire looked as puzzled by that as Gage usually did by Daire's utterances. As he was by the earlier one about Daire *liking* him. Maybe pixies didn't have a word for, well, anything stronger? Because Gage was pretty sure he something stronger-ed Daire.

"I mean, we're hardly on that beach, lying on the soft, caramel-colored sand, stretched out under the sun, feeling the breeze and the salt spray on our...naked bodies, are we?" Daire continued.

His voice had gone low and husky as he painted that picture. That alluring picture of the two of them under that blue sky, serenaded by gently cawing birds, next to the softly lapping ocean. Daire almost sounded like he was working some charm or incantation. Strange. The way he stared hard at Gage was stranger.

"You okay?" Gage asked. "And, no, we're not." Gage took a picture from the wall and passed it to Daire. He scooped up a vase from a plinth. "There. So we look like workers."

"Workers who carry paintings and vases," Daire muttered. He shook his head, as if to clear it and banish the puzzled-seeming crease from his forehead. "Oh, wait, look!"

"What—? Oh." Gage peered at Fang the snoremouse poking its tiny head from Daire's pocket. "What does it mean? Danger, right?"

"I think...that there's another of its kind around? That—" Daire shut up and pressed Gage flat against the wall just as another mouse scurried down the corridor, passing by their feet. "You were right about the surveillance."

"That? Those?" There were at least five, sniffing and squeaking their zigzagging way along.

"Yeah. Floormice. Just freeze. if you don't move, they can't see you," Daire informed him.

"Wish I'd known that beforehand," Gage said through gritted teeth. Then he wouldn't have been standing mostly on one foot, with one hand raised.

"'S'okay. They've gone," Daire said an eternity later, when his hench subsided back into his pocket. Sure enough, tiny mouse-sized snores emerged. "So, up here, right?"

They went up the staircase, Daire juggling the vase from arm to arm. "What would I be doing with this, if I did work here?" he grumbled.

It was Gage's turn to grab at Daire when they reached the landing at the top of the flight of stairs. "There's something..." He felt the presence of something and tilted his head upward. "On the ceiling...spiders?" But he'd seen no cobwebs. "Don't they clean the place better?"

"Not spiders. Spyders." Daire gulped.

"Really?" The small skittering black bodies with their many legs made Gage itch. "Well, let's not give them a chance to spy on us." Inhaling to the fullest extent of his lungs, he blew out a long, hard breath, blasting any clinging arachnid body from its perch above them.

"Nice. I thought it was wyverns who had the magic breath thing?" Daire commented. "What's that, just general griffin power?"

"I guess." Gage tried to look modest. He liked that Daire admired his abilities. "Come on. Should be this main corridor here. And look, more vases all along it." The hallway bore several tables bearing flower-laden pots and jugs. "You can put yours down with them."

"See those flowers? I don't think...I like them," Daire said.

"I know what you mean." Gage squinted at them. They stood tall in their containers, long stems with clusters of round white flowers like fat beads. "Are they berries?"

"How should I know? My bolt hole's never going to grace the cover of *Pixie Home Beautiful*," Daire scoffed.

They might have been berries, but they weren't just white. Gage caught a glimpse of a dark purple dot on one when it moved a little in its vase. And since when did flowers move in their pots?

"Here." Daire grabbed Gage's hand and sucked a finger into his mouth.

"Not now!" Gage protested, although he didn't doubt Daire could persuade him. Even Daire sucking on his finger had him thickening in his pants. Especially Daire sucking on his finger.

"Stars and moon, you're obsessed with sex!" Daire hissed. "Are all griffins this horny all the time or just you?"

"*Me*?" Gage started to protest.

"Right. Well, good to know." Daire smirked, before Gage could protest that Daire was the one who'd taken them to a sex club. Who'd gotten Gage a gig as a stripper. Who'd—

"I was wetting your finger for you to see if there was a breeze along here that was shaking those flower stalks," Daire explained, his eyes wide and his tone injured. He held Gage's hand up in illustration.

Gage registered no coolness on the wetted patch, even when he turned his upraised finger in various directions. Nodding, he took Daire's vase from him and tossed it gently down the corridor. It flew a few yards then landed, rolling along the carpet until it stopped. That was of no concern. What Gage studied was how the bunches of fat round flowers turned to follow it, their deep purple pupils tracking its movement.

"They got eyes?" Daire breathed. "I thought they were creepy."

"It's spyberry," Gage explained, some long-distant lesson or studying coming back to him. "I've never seen the flower, but I know how to manage it." Remaining where he was, he reached out a hand until his fingers touched the nearest display and, wriggling, he was able to pluck the flowers from the jug. "Here." He gave Daire half. "Carry this as we walk past. One bouquet neutralizes another."

"Really? So we just prance down this hallway carrying a bouquet, like brides down an aisle?" Daire didn't look convinced.

"Yes." Gage's mind wanted to dwell on that image, but he didn't let it. "On three. One, two..." On *three* they walked slowly past the vases and pots, and none of the bunches turned to spy on them. Gage let go of Daire's hand — when had he taken it? — to scoop up the vase from where it had rolled against the wall. When they'd walked the gauntlet, he dropped both their bunches of flowers into the container and placed it on the last of the tables.

"Ah, okay. So that's why people carry vases." Daire grinned. "Good thing Griffin Guardians get training about flower arranging. Your workplace must be *sooo* pretty."

Gage narrowed his eyes at him. "Well, time for your pixie powers," he said, indicating the various ornate doors set into the walls of the Holding Suite corridor.

"Yeah. We don't want to get the wrong room and have to pay the ransom for other nappees," Daire replied, moving off.

"We're not paying the ransom for the Storm Queen. We're rescuing her, taking her out of here!" Gage protested.

"How? She must be heavily guarded — they *all* must be," Daire argued. He stopped. "In fact, what *are* we going to do? And how? You do have a plan, right?"

"Right. Right." Gage nodded. A lot.

"You're lying!" Daire accused. "Don't tell me you're just going to wing it."

"Wing it... I was! I am," Gage assured him, thinking on the claw.

"Fly away. *That's* your plan." Daire scoffed, then considered. "Well, it's as good a plan as any, I guess. We'd be in the clear, well away."

There'd still be the matter of the criminals to bring to justice. Gage would have to work out those details. Work them out with Her Majesty. The lack of armed guards struck him. Well, the absence of any guards. Maybe they were all stationed inside the suites?

"Look at this." Daire halted before a door with a parchment bearing a picture of a crown pinned to it. A jade crown. "You thinking what I'm thinking? That with these brains, I should be a Guardian, investigating crimes? Pity you're so speciesist about restricting it to griffins."

"It's called the *Griffin* Guardians," Gage reminded him. "You have your own security force in this realm, the Pixie Patrol, right?" He knew better than to ask if Daire had ever considered joining them. He was probably the sworn enemy of every patrol pixie in the force. They probably all carried his picture for reference. "Look, concentrate."

"I am! And I think it's this one." Daire pressed his ear to the door with the jade crown on it. He hooked his long hair behind his ear to listen better. It revealed the pointed tip, and Gage's mouth dried. "I can't hear anything."

"Then there's unlikely to be a kidnap subject locked in there, trying to tunnel out through the floor or smash the windows," Gage reasoned.

"Yeah. Not *locked* in there, 'cause it's not locked." Daire eased it open a crack and peered in. "It seems occupied though."

"Daire!" Gage's exclamation came too late, as did his grab for the pixie, to stop him sneaking in. "Hells-be-damned, Daire!"

"I think there's someone in bed, through there." Daire pointed.

Somehow, Gage found his hand in Daire's again and they crept slowly and quietly into the bedroom. A woman lay asleep on the bed.

"That her?" Daire asked, whispering into Gage's ear and increasing Gage's arousal.

Gage shrugged. Spotting the firefly lamp, he shook it, to make it light up, ignoring the creatures' annoyed buzzing, then held the lamp high and moved it slowly, so the light fell on the figure.

The woman was tall and slim, with long black hair. Was this her? And was this it, the end to the assignment? The lady, perhaps disturbed by the light or the buzzing, shifted and her hair fell away from her face...revealing elven ears and the royal marking on her forehead centered slightly above the space between her well-arched eyebrows and sharp-pointed ears.

"Your Majesty!" Replacing the lamp, Gage went down on one knee.

She remained asleep.

Daire rolled his eyes at Gage. "Er, Storm Queen?" he said, his voice a little louder.

Nothing happened.

"Your Highness?" Gage's booming voice had her stirring. He only hoped she wouldn't wake up blasting all about her with magic.

She sat up and saw him and shrieked, dragging the bedclothes around her. "Who are you? And you?" She noticed Daire. "You're not my usual attendants. Get out!"

"We're not hotel attendants." Gage hated the uniform. "We're here to rescue you from your kidnappers, Your Majesty." He stood to attention, his left hand on his heart and his right on top of that, as Griffin Guardians did, denoting their pledge to serve

"Majesty? Kidnappers?" The woman's bewildered and alarmed gaze swung between Gage and Daire. "What are you talking about?"

"Look at her!" Daire whispered to Gage. "She really doesn't know why we came here. And worse..."

"She doesn't know who she is," Gage finished for him.

Chapter Nineteen

Maybe Jade was confused because she'd just woken up? Daire could understand that. He often experienced that, especially waking up in a different place. In his case, it was more likely to be under one of the back tables at the Pixie's Neck, or under a row of seats surrounding the porpoise racing pool, his mouth feeling like the inside of one of his boots and his head pounding like someone had hit it, more than once, with one of his boots. But the idea was the same.

"Do you know where you are?" Daire asked Jade, starting small. It helped to get orientated. He waved a hand around the room.

Her dark eyes followed the movement of his hand as if he were a conjurer doing tricks.

"Do you know where you are, *Your Majesty*?" Gage corrected, nudging Daire for his lapse. Daire stumbled, and annoyed, elbowed him back. It had no impact on Gage at all. He could at least pretend.

"Why are you calling me Your Majesty?" Jade sat straighter, perhaps deciding they were no threat. She reached to one then the other bedside firefly lights, shaking them to get them brighter and study her two visitors. "But I believe you have the wrong room."

"Why are you here?" Daire asked, feeling smug. He'd show that griffin he knew how to conduct an investigation! "My Lady," he added. Calling someone lord or lady — he couldn't go wrong there.

"Yes, that's my title. I'm the Lady Janeth. I'm an elf," the Storm Queen said.

Daire studied her. She didn't seem to be telling a lie.

"And you're here for…" Gage prompted.

"I asked that!" Daire protested, as if they were keeping score.

"I'm getting married soon!" 'Lady Janeth' blushed. "It's going to be a rather lavish affair, and I'm here in this spa for the bride-to-be pamper package."

Ah. Okay… As far as Daire knew, the Storm Queen was already hitched, to an orc. Which was what this was all about. He did a double take — Gage was in his official Griffin Guardians uniform. Well, two could play at that game…

"Why are you disrobing in my room?" 'Lady Janeth' hissed.

"Security," Daire replied, settling his white shirt. "We're security, I mean. Could you tell us a little bit more about why you're here?

'Lady Janeth' did, describing the place's aromatherapy massage and herbology facial and elemental sauna. Oh, and the leisure facilities the spa boasted, which included a relaxation pool, an invigoration pool and a swimming pool. "I haven't tried that one yet," she confessed.

Gage nodded as she enthused about the salt scrub and the butter moisturizing. When she described the steam treatment, all Daire could think was that if they sprinkled pepper on her too, she'd be perfectly seasoned and cooked.

Jade moved on to enthuse about the beauty treatments on offer.

"Oh, a matching pedicure as well?" Gage faked interest in the foot Jade stuck out of the sheets. "While you enjoy a light meal. I see. One moment, your ladyship."

He drew Daire aside. "This is serious," he whispered, jerking his head

"This is actually a good business model." Daire considered. "A good way to hold kidnapped people while waiting for ransom. I wonder if they bill the rescuer for the cost of the stay and treatments? Because, according to this parchment of what's on offer, they make a paste out of rolled gold and rub it into the skin. Says here it brightens you. That can't come cheap."

"Daire, focus! The Storm Queen's helpless. Well, sitting up in bed brushing her hair. But she has no memory!" Gage hissed.

"That's what I mean. If victims don't remember, they can't say exactly where they were after they get released, or who did it, right? They can't lead authorities here." Although Daire doubted any realm had an extradition treaty with this place. It was what the territory was all about. "But more importantly, if the person doesn't know they're napped, they won't try to fight back or escape." He gave a low whistle of admiration.

"The things you don't find morally repugnant worry me," Gage replied after a pause.

"Look, I'm not saying I approve." Daire jabbed him with a finger. Because he didn't, did he? He was hardly planning to replicate this on a smaller, dingier scale, in his bolt hole or in one of the rooms that could be hired out at the Cockpit. "I'm just saying one can admire a clever business plan. The artistry. Gage!"

He didn't want the griffin shifter to think badly of him. Which annoyed him. "I'm here to rescue her," he reminded Gage.

After a moment of searching his eyes, Gage gave a short nod. "Can you break the spell?"

"You think she's under a *charm*?" Daire considered. "I don't think that can be how this is done. It would take so much magic to bespell not just Jade but all the victims, either one after the other or at the same time, depending on the schedule, that there'd be traces everywhere. Like loose droppings, you know?"

"Charming."

"And—" Daire stopped. "Did you just make a joke? Fancy that. I didn't think Guardians could, in uniform." That Gage donned whenever he could, like armor. "It would be detected. Like, that elemental they keep on hand—and they must have more than one about the place—would be going buzzing mad."

"At all the loose droppings, yes." Gage nodded. He looked back at Jade, who was selecting a sleep mask from a box of them. "So you think her food or food and drink's drugged?"

Daire went to peer at Jade. "Her eyes are bright and she seems alert and aware," he said softly, coming back. "Giving tranquilizing potions could be risky, long-term, and what kind of root or leaf or seed could empty her being and replace it with a fake one?"

"Maybe something in a cosmetic? A cream or powder?" With a sharp head bow to Jade, Gage charged into the bathroom.

Daire understood that Gage wanted to find what was keeping Jade in this condition, but he doubted whatever it was would be that easy to find, along with a box next to it marked *antidote.* "Gage. Gage!" He yanked at Gage's arm, stopping him from ransacking the jars and boxes. "The same idea would apply, that she'd be groggy and dazed, and she isn't."

Gage stood back and shook unguent from his fingers. "Thanks," he muttered, not meeting Daire's eyes when Daire passed him a towel. "So what do you think?"

Daire shoved a stopper back in a vial. "I think she's probably hypnotized."

"Oh!" Gage sprinted back into the bedroom.

Jade, who was lying down again, sat up and barely muffled a shriek.

"Please..." Daire indicated she should relax again. All the exertion and strain couldn't be good for her, in her blessed condition. "Now, there'd need to be an amulet or some object about her, or on her, at all time, that's like the..."

"Repository? Reservoir?" Gage suggested, when Daire was trying to think of the word.

"Gizmo that keeps the power close to her, yeah."

They both looked Jade over. She wore no jewelry, no rings or earrings. Not at the moment, but Daire would bet she had plenty. So many she wouldn't miss one, or a couple... "All right!" he muttered, when Gage glared at him. "I'm just thinking that she must change things up. It's not like she's a peasant with just a joining ring, or a love-me-knot necklace, you know?"

"So the one thing that's on her all the time..." Gage spoke slowly as he trailed his gaze up Jade, to bring it to rest where Daire's was.

"Her elf mark," they said at the same time.

Daire reached out a gentle finger. He'd seen the marks in pictures and at a distance, but not this close, and didn't know enough about them to tell what the bits of the design meant about her family tree. Well, she was the ruler, so hers must be top of the heap. The biggest, or blackest, or deepest, or whatever.

The mark was raised from the skin but was very much a part of an elf's body…and couldn't be removed.

"We don't know enough about what we're doing to try to get it off her." He swallowed.

"But I do know, well, okay, *think*, it's a transceiver." Gage looked at him. "I've been thinking about all the surveillance, the statues, the birds… This realm, over the rainbow, seems to be run like that."

"And this hotel. The spyders, floormice…" *And those creepy plants with eyes.* Daire shuddered.

"So it must all feed back somewhere. To a control room."

Daire understood that. Most gaming rooms he'd been in had a control area behind the space where the action went down. This here would be no different, only the area would be more removed, not next door to this suite. "So you think if we find it and what, smash it to pieces, then all this will be broken?"

"Yes. Well, I think it's worth a try."

Gage was honest.

"I bet I know where it is. Reception!" Daire exclaimed. "The people who monitor who comes in and out of a venue know everything *and* control everything that goes on. Come on! Oh, and better put your doorman's clothes on again." He enjoyed saying that. Gage did and they set off, as quickly as was safe.

"That dome's got to have something to do with it." In the atrium, Daire tilted back to look up. What did it put him in mind of? "As above, so below," he muttered, eyeing the circular reception counter, placed directly under the dome.

"Circles are said to be powerful shapes," Gage muttered, walking around the counter...and finding nothing.

"Walk the other way around it," Daire suggested.

Gage did so and— "Still nothing." Gage glared at him.

Daire shrugged. "Worth a try."

But all their tapping and rapping and thumping, their stroking, pushing and shoving, on the marble countertop and around its sides, both inside and outside, produced nothing. Daire raised his head at the small taps that continued. *Footsteps.*

"Someone's coming!" he whispered. "Quick, over there to that wall, look."

"Got it." Gage rushed him over and slammed his body into Daire's, effectively hiding him, then bent down to kiss him. A lot.

Daire initially struggled, then went with it. Gage was a good kisser, his tongue seeking and finding and taking and giving. Peeping around the edge of Gage's face, Daire saw the suit approaching. One of the door porters—

"Gaston!" the doorman rebuked.

—who presumed Gage was one of them.

"You've been warned about this," the hotel employee continued. He tsked. "One more complaint about your roving hands and wandering tongue, and you'll be whistling out your ass for your bonus this year. So think on."

178

Shaking his head, he continued on his way. Daire nudged Gage when it was safe for them to disengage and adjust themselves.

"As I was saying," Daire continued, licking at the taste of Gage in his mouth, "there's a maintenance door here. It must lead somewhere that can help us." Hiding his smile at Gage's rueful expression, Daire shouldered the door open and ducked to go through it.

Thankfully, the utility tunnel they found on the other side of it was a little wider and higher. Small holes were set in one of its sides here and there and various pipes ran along its floor, water supply and trash removal the two most obvious. They rounded a corner and Gage covered his nose "Whoa. Is it the trash that stinks?"

"No. It's the sewer." Gagging, Daire pointed an elbow at the open channel set along one side of the tunnel. Dirty water ran sluggishly through it. "I'm just happy it's so late, and people probably won't be using the"—a dull flushing sound made him stop—"facilities," he finished. "Oh, gods of gods..."

A small brown something plopped from a hole in the wall just near them and landed in the water.

"Oh, that's disgusting," Gage moaned.

"Think that's bad?" Daire flattened them both against the wall, away from the sewer just before a wet, sticky, smelly, lumpy brown animal, looking like the item that had just dropped into its home, roared up from the trough of water and fell upon its 'food', devouring it with gusto. Then a long brown tongue, as lumpy and wet as the rest of its body, came out to lick what was probably its mouth.

"That's..." Gage held a hand over his mouth, his shoulders heaving. "I don't have words to describe that. Whatever it is."

"A Schmutzbeast." Daire had seen them in the bowels of a very rich, well-appointed home once.

"But their appearance...and stench!" Gage shuddered.

"Yeah, it proves the old adage, you are what you eat. Come on." Daire set his best foot forward.

Carefully.

Chapter Twenty

Gage forced back another heave — Griffin Guardians didn't toss their cookies on an assignment. It made him stumble and his hand knocked into a large pipe. Hissing at the pain, he yanked his hand away. "Watch out. These gray ones are scalding hot." They had tiny holes along their length, like pinpricks, for the steam to escape.

Vapor hissed out in release from an aperture that was bigger than the rest, and Daire, a little farther ahead, whipped around at the noise. Doing that on wet, uneven ground had him slipping and skidding, toward an open pool of water at the top of the pipe. A hazy heat cloud hung over it...because the water was boiling.

"*No!*" Gage exclaimed as if the power of his voice could halt Daire's arm-waving, leg-arching fall. Time was supposed to stand still here but Gage didn't think it had because it slackened now, allowing him to see Daire in clear, slow motion, about to land in water that would scorch the skin from his bones.

"No," Gage repeated, simply, and without him thinking about it, popped out a wing and folded it around Daire, wrapping him in his quills a mere feathersbreadth from the boiling surface of the water. A quick curl of his feathers and Daire was whisked from the trough to stand beside him, unharmed. Only when Daire's feet touched the ground did Gage unfurl his wing, He had to shake it out, trying not to exclaim where the steam had wilted it.

"Gage..." Daire's face had too many emotions on it for Gage to understand all at once.

"Are you hurt?" they both asked at the same time, then both shook their heads.

"Would you...?" Daire swallowed, compressed his lips, then spoke. "Hold me? Like this, but more...in both wings?"

Oh. He'd never done that before. Never part-shifted, never enveloped another person to him in his wings. But he was now, holding Daire close to his heart, that Daire must be able to feel thumping where his head was pressed to Gage's chest.

Gage wallowed in the feeling, that *acceptance*, and wanted more. Daire had seen him shift, in the Double J club, and been turned on by Gage's griffin form. Seduction was one thing. And Daire had been happy to be seated on Gage's back and be flown by his griffin form. A winged creature was useful. But just to be with him, like that? Gage wanted it as he didn't remember wanting anything before. Slowly, Daire raised his head and looked Gage right in the eyes, and it was as if he were narrowcasting to Gage, "*Do it. Please.*"

He would. He was. The hands Gage had looped around Daire's lower back became claws, the forefeet of the griffin. The legs Gage stood on became a lion's hindquarters. His tail emerged and wrapped around Daire, holding him tight with that too. He wasn't sure how long they stood there, with Daire nestled to him, but it felt so good. So right. He rested his beak on the top of Daire's head, making him squirm and burrow closer, which made Gage warble a laugh.

A tear slid from Gage's eye onto Daire's head, and Daire stirred. Gage let him stand upright on his own, and shifted back, to stand there in his other form. Daire reached out a hand and stroked his face, running his thumb along the cheekbone.

"Next time, I'll learn the feel of you in your griffin form," he promised. "When we have time. Which we don't now."

Daire was right. This wasn't the time or place for anything like this. *Like what?* Gage asked himself. *So intimate. So shattering.* He nodded. "It must be this way."

It was, and they only had one further adventure, a run-in with water elementals, on the way to the door helpfully marked *Control Room.*

"So, how are we handling this?" Daire whispered.

"Like this. Stand back." Gage took in a deep breath, centering himself, then burst through the door. Normally he'd have shouted, "Griffin Guardians!" along with his title, his business and the code of federal law that empowered him to act. Now, he moved swiftly and silently, surprising the two guards dozing in front of viewing screens.

They didn't even get the chance to spin around in their chairs before Gage had dealt both of them blows to the head that knocked them unconscious. Gage didn't have his equipment with him, so finding suitable material to tie the pair up with made him take longer than he normally would have at something like this, but in no time at all the duo was strapped to their chairs, bound and gagged.

"Griffin power." Daire nodded approval. "And I'm a little bit suspicious of your ease with ropes and gags."

He paused, and Gage felt that whatever he wanted to say had nothing to do with the situation at hand. "Things...will have to keep for later," he told him. "For when this is over."

Daire hesitated a little longer then gave a nod. Gage burned to know what the pixie wanted to say but tamped it down. "Focusing on the assignment is the right thing to do," he continued, more to himself, truth be told.

Daire shrugged, looking like a caricature of a pixie, an exaggeration that other species imitated. He joined Gage in searching the room and especially the control panel. It was way beyond anything Gage had ever seen. The HQ didn't have this level of equipment. He peered helplessly at the buttons and speakers.

"I think you were right just now." Daire jerked his thumb at the tied-up guards. "The direct approach is the best." He hit a button marked *Override* and spoke in a bland sing-song delivery. "Would the kidnappers of Jade, the Storm King, also known as the Storm Queen, please go to the control room at once. That's the kidnappers of Jade, the Storm King or Queen, to the control room now. Thank you." He took his hand off the button and shrugged again.

"I wish Brackish and Clove were here," he said.

"Who? Why?" Gage's heart trip-trapped, and not just at Daire's bold move. He half-wished they weren't talking, so he could focus on this. "Why?" He'd already asked that.

"Some pixie friends of mine," Daire explained. "Because they'd have a bet on how quickly someone comes in and who it is. Like, five coins says it's those cousins and seven coins says they're here within five minutes. You know?"

It was Gage's turn to shrug this time. "Stand back," he said. "Let me handle—"

"Not this time. Why should you have all the fun?" Daire protested, following Gage to stand to one side of the closed door.

"*Fun?*" Gage shut up at the running footsteps outside. Whoever it was must be a guest in the hotel too. He readied himself.

"Told you!" Daire yelled when the door pushed open and two male elves hurried in. They both had long dark hair and similar enough features to Jade for him to declare with confidence, "Jaxon, Jaleb, do come in!" He didn't introduce himself but leapt on the nearest one and headbutted him in the stomach then started kicking him in the shins and stamping on his feet when the elf staggered backward and smashed into the wall. As soon as the elf splayed out, his hands flinging to his sides at the impact, Daire kicked him in the nuts. This brought the elf's head down, him trying to curl into a protective ball, which was when Daire smashed his forehead into the elf's nose.

"Stars on a platter!" Gage exclaimed, pulling the prisoner he'd subdued more cleanly, quietly and less violently away from the hopping, sobbing, yelping mess Daire had made of his cousin. "Which one are you? And no, we're not taking bets on it." That last was to Daire.

"Jaxon," gasped the elf, his head turned so not all of it was slammed into the wall with the rest of the front of his body.

"He looks more like a Jaleb," Daire commented, giving another kick to the actual Jaleb, who raised his head and looked over Daire's shoulder.

"Help us," he groaned.

"Help you?" Daire asked incredulously. "Why...? Ah. You're talking to someone who's come in and is standing behind me, aren't you? Behind us." He flicked a glance at Gage, by his side.

Gage didn't need to see Jaleb's nod, or the way Jaxon signaled with his eyes to that someone. Who was it?

"Usually..." Daire gulped and continued, "it's the person nearest to the victim who stands to gain, so they're the one who's responsible."

"Well..." Gage was the trained investigator here, the one with the theoretical learning and practical experience.

"Now, Jade's married, so, my big question here..." Daire was still speaking. "Is are we gonna turn around and be facing an orc? 'Cause kicking an elf in the 'nads is one thing, but an orc? I don't even know where their balls are. Do you?"

"No!" Gage protested. "How would I?"

"From your training!" Daire spared him a glance. "Don't you have to learn all about different species to be a federal agent?"

"Not their nuts," Gage protested.

"But I don't think it's an orc." Daire breathed in. *"There's no smell."* He whispered the last bit.

"Let me —" Gage started.

"If the next two words you intend to say are 'handle it', think again," Daire warned him.

"But..." He didn't want Daire getting hurt. Couldn't bear even the idea.

"On three. We turn around on three," Daire announced. "Okay? Not you." He stamped again on the elf's foot. "You know, I see why that Clubfoot chaun likes this. So, one, two—"

"Three." Gage gave a final wrench to his prisoner's shoulder socket and turned.

It wasn't an orc called Grlind who stood there, green-skinned, lumpy-pated and fanged-teethed. It wasn't an orc at all. Instead, it was an elderly elf, one who looked less stooped and dried-up than when they'd spoken to him last. Yesterday? Earlier? Gage wasn't sure anymore.

He wasn't flapping about and twittering, wracked with shock and nerves. It *was* the same councilor or advisor that they'd met, but now he stood upright, looking in control and confident, even a little bit powerful.

"Ah. You know, we never did get his name?" Daire commented.

Chapter Twenty-One

"This kinda distinguished guy, we never got his name," Daire clarified, looking the elf up and down.

Gage thought they must have, or it must be in the information parchments he had as part of his assignment.

"Murstyn," replied the elf, giving them the smallest of down-and-up head nods. Even his voice was different. Richer. Deeper. His 'old kook' persona had been just that, a veneer. *A disguise.*

"Murstyn…" Gage tried it out. Did it seem a little bit familiar? He ran it and the elf's face against any wanted criminals or fugitives the Guardians were currently tracking or on alert for, and came up blank. But something wasn't right here. He moved slightly to keep the cousins in his line of sight along with Murstyn.

"Or full title, Murstyn the Silver Fox?" Daire asked with a wink. "Love that suit. Betting you didn't get that at In The Closet. Tailor-made?"

"Daire!" Gage gave a jerk of his head toward Jaxon and Jaleb, who were helping each other stand upright, trying to show Daire that the three elves were linked, and not just by species.

"What? I can admire good tailoring, can't I?" Daire asked. "So, anyway, we caught the naughty parties for you."

"*Guilty* parties," Gage corrected. Two of which were sneering at him now, while their third stood silent, probably trying to read them, as Gage was him.

"Funny, I thought you'd be all 'thank you, thank you! The elven kingdom's ruler is safe thanks to you!'" Daire continued, waving his hands, his voice chirpy. "You know, offering rewards in gratitude for the service..."

Gage really hoped the inklings of suspicion glinting here and there in relation to the pixie were fool's gold, nothing of note.

"Catching traitors whose actions would have destabilized a realm, and all that." Daire ground his toe into the floor, his hands behind his back.

"Daire..." Gage said again.

He didn't know what Daire was up to and didn't like not knowing. On the surface, it seemed Daire was hinting about a payment for apprehending Jaxon and Jaleb. This in itself was contrary to every tenant of law enforcement, the wrongness of it making Gage's nape itch.

But beyond that, didn't Daire understand the connection between the elves? Between the hired hands or figureheads and the one pulling their strings? Couldn't he see that the elderly elf who stood silent and watchful, demonstrating decades of sizing people up for their triggers and marshaling his resources to pull them, was heavily involved in this affair?

Or maybe Daire did, because it could look like Daire was angling for a different kind of reward, for performing a different kind of service, still connected to the kidnap and attempt to depose the Storm King.

No. Gage shrugged off the icy drops down the back of his neck that had taken over from the itch. He was choosing to believe Daire hadn't comprehended. And so he'd make him.

"Stay where you are," he warned the traitor cousins. "You should know that I'm a federal law enforcement officer. It means I do this for a living. Usually at this stage, when the criminal is unmasked"—he gave a slight motion toward Murstyn, like a teaching aid for Daire—"people are gasping out 'why'? 'Why did you do this?' But I won't be asking that."

He paced up and down a little, as he tended to when giving talks or instructing or questioning. "Prajg," he said. "It's always prajg."

Daire giggled and put his hand over his mouth.

"Excuse me?" Gage glared at him.

"S-sorry." Daire wiped his eyes. "I just didn't know you knew pixie sex slang…or that that was what you were in the mood for! And I never thought you were into foreskin play, with you not having one? Or d'you mean it's a sex act you like to watch? Well, each to his own."

"Wh-what?" Gage stammered in confusion.

"Prajg. It's when a male inserts his glans into the foreskin of another penis for some mutual, well…" Daire mimed thrusting. "Hey, no judgment here." He raised his hands, palms out.

"Prajg—" Gage waited for Daire's snickers to stop. "Is an acronym to help law enforcement learn the motives for committing crimes. It stands for greed, anger, jealousy, revenge and pride."

Daire raised a hand. "They're in a different order," he pointed out.

"They're in order of importance. Of how frequently they feature, while the acronym was coined as being easier to remember," Gage replied, his teeth gritted. He inhaled, getting back on track. "And of course, the next big question is what makes people commit crimes. And no, what makes them isn't the same as why. In asking what leads them, we're dealing with the background. The bigger picture. And it's dalpp."

"What? It's not!" Daire protested.

"*Dalpp!*" Gage repeated louder.

"My cousin, Dalpp? He's harmless! Useless, even!" Daire protested. "He couldn't make a pig roll in shit, as the saying goes. And he's tried, during that pig-training job he briefly had. *Oof.* Stank to high heavens he did, for that whole week. In a different way to how he does normally, I mean. He's not the cleanest of pixies, as things go, you know?"

"Poverty," Gage began.

"Well, he's not rich," Daire agreed. "None of us are. But we get by." He winked.

"Poverty, parental neglect, low self-esteem, alcohol and drug abuse. Dalpp." Gage rushed them all out in one breath. He wondered if he'd have any enamel left on his teeth when this was over, he was grinding them so hard.

"Ahem." Murstyn's fake cough brought their attention to him. "As entertaining as this is…"

"It's not entertaining. It's serious," Gage protested.

"I'm with the well-dressed elf. Can we move it along?" Daire asked.

"Fine!" Gage snapped. "So we come to the triangle. Which is not a deviant sex act."

Jaxon raised his hand. "It...is, actually."

"Yeah," Jaleb agreed.

"Oh, I know! Is it when two males and one — ?"

"It's the three factors that create a criminal offense," Gage yelled over Daire. "One. The desire of a criminal to commit a crime. Two. The target of the criminal's desire. Three. The opportunity for the crime to be committed."

"Dot." Daire nodded. "That would make an easy acronym to remember that."

It will, actually. He should remember that. Pass it along. He gave a sharp nod of thanks to Daire. "And these three items are all met here." Gage swept a hand around. "And they lead me to the crime in progress here. Murstyn the silver fox — I mean Murstyn the elf, in accordance with regulation twelve, sub-section three, I am empowered to bring you to Griffin Guardians HQ for questioning in regards to..."

How complicated it all was washed over him. The assignment he'd been given was guard duty. No abduction had been reported and so no authorization to investigate one had been granted. In addition, when reporting in, Gage had failed to mention the slight kidnapping turn the mission had taken.

The way Murstyn stood there, tapping that elegant cane he carried and raising one well-groomed eyebrow said he knew as much.

"Oh fuck it! You kidnapped the Storm Queen!" Gage burst out. "And I'm gonna throw the book at you!" And gods in a cave, he might as well have added *so there* on the end. He hadn't — he hoped — but the words rang around the control room, just like the slam of a stamped foot did, and he hadn't done that either.

"*Gage!*" Daire tipped his head, indicating he wanted Gage to step closer to speak privately to him. "He *works* for the Storm Queen! He's a trusted councilor or advisor or aide or something, part of the *royal court!*" He whispered — loudly — from behind his hand as if embarrassed by what he was saying, flickering his gaze to Murstyn, his expression apologetic.

Gage gaped at Daire. The Pixies Lands didn't have a ruling family, and Daire was so far removed from the machinery of power — except when it came after him — that he probably didn't know how it corrupted. How being close to it could make a person want more, then lust for more, until that craving burned away all noble, good emotions, leaving the person an empty husk, pushing for ever-higher positions, consumed by their desire to be at the very top.

"He wouldn't do that," Daire finished, his voice loud and confident. He made a rueful face at the councilor.

"But—" Gage started. He was reluctant to burst Daire's bubble.

"But I did do that," Murstyn bragged.

And *pop*. Bubble burst.

"Oh?" As usual, Daire didn't sound disgusted at the mention of something morally repugnant. He seemed interested. Fascinated, even. Gage fought the sinking in his chest. "And why would a councilor do that?"

Murstyn scoffed. He looked around, and Jaxon staggered over to the chairs, tipped a still-unconscious security guard from one and brought it over to him. Murstyn undid the buttons on his suit jacket, pulled at the knees of his pants and sat. "My name isn't Jaxon or

Jaleb," he began. "It isn't Jerrick or Jomb, or Joziah or Jareth. What does that tell you?"

"Hm." Daire rubbed his chin. He signaled to Jaleb who copied his cousin and fetched Daire a seat, clearing it for him. "Seeing a bit of a theme with the names," he said.

"Yes, all members of all royal-adjacent families' names begin with the letter Jule." Murstyn sneered, directing it over to the two cousins. "I'll never be on that level, despite having more foresight than Jerrick, or more ability than Jomb, or better ideas than Joziah or Jareth put together!"

"Yeah, but you're Murstyn, the best shagger in the elven kingdom!" Daire waved a hand at him. "I've heard of you—I remember now! Pixies come back to the Lands from your realm walking bow-legged and can't sit for a week after a good hard fuck with you at the tavern where you keep a room and…" He slowed, perhaps trying to reconcile the picture of a sexual athlete with the elderly elf in front of him. "Ah. Not you?"

From the explosion and tirade that followed, Gage understood that these feats were not performed by Murstyn but by a dissolute elf called Jagger, who used Murstyn's name when he committed deviant, perverted, immoral sexual acts with creatures from other realms and kingdoms. Again, Daire looked more approving than repulsed.

"And I don't even know what baking brownie batter is!" Murstyn finished in a burst of thunder.

Gage…had heard of it. And the thought of this elf indulging in it—

"Oh, think that's funny, do you?" Murstyn caught the expression Gage couldn't hide quickly enough.

"Well, laugh at this, Captain." He moved his hand to the inside pocket of his jacket, and Gage went into a ready position...for the letter the elf held out to him.

"I have been in communication with your commander," Murstyn explained as Gage scanned the parchment. "So you're not only back on active duty, you have a promotion coming, Captain Gage. Or should I say—"

"*Major*?" Gage read.

"And you're in line for a transfer." Murstyn produced a second sheaf of parchment. "This is a letter of request written by Her Highness."

"Well, it's on official palace paper, at least," Daire commented, reading at Gage's elbow. "Sun in a bucket, look at all those big words—exceptional, extraordinary, exemplary... Seems she got stuck on E. Oh no, here's punctilious, particular, punctual... Nice."

Murstyn shrugged, failing to look modest.

"To be the Guardians' permanent detachment to the elven kingdom, based at the Storm King's palace?" Gage looked up, not understanding.

"That should be painless. Plain sailing. Piece of cake." Daire grinned, his green eyes shining. "Would it come with a grand apartment in the palace and an even grander pile of gold, now?"

"Oh yes." Murstyn nodded. "You'd have all that. You...as in you two." He waved a finger from Gage to Daire.

"*What*?" Gage staggered.

"Gage!" Daire's eyes glittered.

"You'd *like* that?" Gage asked.

"Well duh! Gage, it would be a way to be together!" Daire grabbed his hand. "Which is currently impossible with your job, our different lives, you being a griffin shifter, me being a pixie, you being tall, me being short... You know, you can stop me anytime."

"To be together..." Gage whispered, staring at Daire.

"Because we're, well, in *like*," Daire whispered back. "And, truth be told, I think bonded?"

Gage's world rocked.

Chapter Twenty-Two

Gage actually thought he might stagger and fall. *In like as in love, yes.* He'd dared to think, to hope, that. But *soul-joined*, if that was what Daire meant, that...wasn't something he wanted thrown at him in front of other people, criminals he was attempting to bring to justice, in fact, oh, and for preference, not in the middle of an assignment!

"B-bonded?" he tried to clarify.

"Yeaaahh. I can sort of help myself to your strength for my own purposes—don't get mad—and I think you're getting some of my smarts." Daire preened.

"Smarts? From Little Mr. 'That's the Storm King's councilor—what's he doing here?'" mocked Jaxon.

"Shut it or I'll have you in the stocks!" Daire told him. "Can I do that, Murstyn?"

"To the ruler? One...*shouldn't*," Murstyn replied. "But what if the ruler were in the stocks and citizens were charged money to pelt him, or them?"

He smiled in a creepy way at the cousins, leaving Gage in no doubt as to who the power behind the throne would be.

"See what I mean about my wonderful, progressive without being too touchy-feely and gods forbid, 'inclusive' ideas?" Murstyn preened even harder than Daire.

"Nice one! You could charge an entrance fee to the arena, then charge separately for the missiles, which have to be purchased on site. Domates, egges, dung patties..." Daire smiled. "But, Gage, haven't you noticed a benefit to being with me? And not just this luscious pixie body?"

Gage remained silent. He wouldn't mention that he was seeing colors. He needed more time to check into that. Because it might not be...what Daire was saying. Ten minutes ago, the idea that he and Daire were soul-joined would have thrilled him. But now, seeing Daire like this... A chill went through him.

"Say something!" Daire commanded.

Gage tried, but nothing came out

"Gage, this would give us a chance. Give us a fantastic start!" Daire coaxed.

"Daire." Gage wondered if his heart was actually breaking. "This isn't possible. At all. It goes against everything I believe in!"

"Like duty and service, that you prefer over life, never mind love. And of course you wouldn't take a chance on a pixie, would you?" Daire replied. "I know what your species believes. That pixies are shifty. That we're all ne'er-do-wells, cheaters and thieves, and that I'm the worst of the lot."

"You're not." Gage knew that, at least. "But how much of this new life is just you wanting a new start? Moving to another realm, away from things here?"

"His debts. His creditors," Murstyn threw in.

"Yes, I know!" Gage snapped.

"I can't believe you asked that!" Daire gasped.

But Gage noticed he didn't answer.

"So if you don't intend to take up the offer—"

"Hey, no one's said no yet!" Daire interrupted Murstyn.

"Might I inquire as to your next move? Going back to the HQ and denouncing me? Because I doubt you'd be believed." Murstyn looked smug. "I have almost a century's service to the Storm lineage."

Gage didn't have a next move planned, and Daire seemed to read this in Gage's face. "We'll think of something," he assured Gage. "We work well together. Our strengths combine."

"Or you help yourself to his!" Jaleb snorted.

"It's the stocks for you, too, when I'm an advisor. Or attaché. Or envoy. I haven't decided on my role yet," Daire promised him. He gazed at Gage as if he could persuade him to change his mind.

But Gage couldn't. He shook his head, telling Daire in more than his words of a moment ago that the proposal was impossible for him to accept.

"Oh, I almost forgot. In addition to something for Captain Gage, I have a little trifle for Daire the pixie," Murstyn said, holding out several small sheaves of paper to him.

Daire looked up from them, blinking. "But these are my chits."

Murstyn nodded. "I bought up your markers. Including your biggest one. Quite the losses you've had!"

"From Monops? I don't believe it." Daire was almost open-mouthed.

"I thought you might say that." Murstyn again reached a hand into his pocket, and brought out a small device, something like a tube, or a telescope. "It's an eyespyglass with speaking channel. You know what they are? I will get Mr. Monops for you…"

It took a while, but eventually Monops' voice came from the device. "Is this on? Can you hear me? I hate these things. Always go off when I'm on the crapper."

Murstyn passed it over to Daire and indicated he should hold it to his eye and let the attachment dangle to his ear.

"Ah. Daire. This elf paid your chit. We're all square. Now fuck off and leave me to take a dump in peace," Monops greeted him.

Daire handed the glass back. "Well, thanks, Murstyn. Much appreciated."

"What's the catch?" Gage demanded.

"No catch. All you have to do is ignore this." Murstyn gestured at himself and the other two elves.

"Ignore a crime? No way. Elves Murstyn, Jaxon and Jaleb, I hereby —"

"Okay."

"*What?*" Gage broke off at Daire's one-word answer.

"I said okay. It's fine by me." Daire took a step toward the elves. "What? You expect me to play the hero? I'm not a griffin. I'm a pixie. Pixies gonna pixie, right?"

Gage's heart broke a little.

"Yep, pixies are always gonna be good-for-nothing, lazy, shiftless—stop me any time," Daire said.

"Stop— I have to stop them," Gage answered. "Even if that means taking you in too." His heart cracked a little more.

"How? You got a plan, *Guardian*?" Daire inquired. "Or were you going with brute force again, like, oh, I don't know, yanking us all back over the rainbow?"

Gage...had been thinking that.

"And risk the Storm Queen's pregnancy?" Murstyn tsked.

"You want ideas, you come to me," Daire said...to Murstyn. "Seems to me you need a fixer. And so happens, I'm for hire." His grin looked like a pixie *Wanted* poster.

"Then I have no choice." Gage's heart broke the rest of the way as he made his decision. Daire, angry that Gage wouldn't abandon everything to be with him, had turned against him. and would have to be treated as such. Gage would have to confess all to Commander Slate and that would be the end of him as a Guardian, but tough. Right had to win.

He sent out the special whistle to the papagae network. Being supra-beings, they could access all realms. *Does that include this one?* He'd soon see. With a bang, one appeared in the air near him....and headed straight for Daire when the pixie whistled.

"What...?" Gage struggled to summon the bird back, but couldn't. "Daire, what are you doing?"

"Helping myself to your power to cast magic." Daire gave a cheeky grin. "And I'm thinking we can use this official avian to spread the word that the Storm Queen's missing and that the Guardian guarding her deserted his post. Let people add two and two together themselves, you know?"

"You mean pin this on the griffin?" Jaxon asked.

Daire shrugged. "*I* didn't say that. You did."

"Underhand. Cruel. Sneaky. I like it," Murstyn declared.

"Knew you would. What say we go grab lots of stupidly big cocktails by the pool and talk about my salary package and palace apartments?" His arms around all three elves' shoulders and an official papagai on his, Daire steered the group out. He spared a glimpse back at Gage then faced forward again. "And you let me handle it?" And the three were gone.

No. No. That doesn't — That isn't... But it had. It was. *Pixies are tricky, remember?* he admonished himself. "Pixies are pricks!" he cried. He'd been right to think so. A noise from the security guards he'd knocked out made him remember to untie them before he left the room. He wanted to get out of there, the place where Daire the pixie had, well, pixied.

Gage had no idea where he was going, in his sad wander through the hotel until he found a door to the outside. He stumbled over paths and lawns, scenes of his time together with Daire playing through his head. Their first meeting, with its heated argument and passionate sex. At the pixie club, Daire teaching him to dance, and Gage dancing — for Daire. How much it had aroused Daire. Their last-minute escape, on the back of a stolen horse, which had led to then finding out vital information. How Daire's actions had gotten them over the rainbow.

"*Pixies gonna pixie,*" Daire had said. But he was so much more than a stereotype. So much more than his twinkling green eyes, unruly chestnut hair, snub little nose and pointed ears. It was his quick mind and lively spirit that had won Gage. Daire had pulled Gage from his shades-of-gray world, his narrow-focus existence, and taken him on the adventure that was life.

Took me for a ride, Gage told himself. *And now I'm left here, stranded, alone.* Even if he and Daire were soul-joined, Daire hadn't given a toss about it, or Gage, choosing his old life and ways. Which Gage would have to do, too. Would have to forget Daire, with his lightning mind and gift for improvising a way out of the situations he…got himself…into…

Gage's brain felt far from lightning, the way it stuttered to a stop. Daire was used to thinking on the run. Coming up with plans to save the day. "*And you let me handle it?*" That phrase… Had that been a message to Gage, who'd said that on a couple of occasions? Gage had to believe it was!

And even if it wasn't, he had to speak to Daire. He couldn't leave matters like that. Not when Daire had opened his heart to Gage and confessed his feelings. Gage owed it to Daire to let him know that those feelings— "That I love him," Gage said. He only hoped it wasn't too late. How long had he been meandering, lost in the doldrums of his thoughts?

Long enough for the day to have started, the warm sun and pretty colors and scents from the flowers climbing the trellises and growing in the bushes enticing people to be up and about already. Gage didn't spare any time and attention for that. He was too busy finding a hotel employee tall and broad enough that Gage could steer him away to a quiet corner, knock him unconscious and steal his uniform.

What would Daire do? Gage used that as his guide so that instead of bursting up to the quartet enjoying drinks around a table next to the pool, he hovered at the tables behind them, making sure the elves' backs were to him.

"One cosmopixieton, and one brownie libre," he said to the breakfasting couple he was serving, placing their drinks down for them.

Daire looked up and their eyes locked. Neither did anything, just stared at the other until a grin spread over Daire's face, matching the one Gage knew was crossing his. A gentle tickle stroked from the inside of his head down his breastbone, to his stomach. It wasn't like the rumbling almost-pain he'd felt a couple of times before, but he now knew it meant Daire was tapping into his strength and power. *He's welcome. Because we're bonded.*

An observer might have thought elves couldn't hold their drinks, because the three at the table next to the water were growing more relaxed and expansive by the minute. But observers wouldn't know that Daire was casting a charm or maybe laying a compulsion, now Gage was here, loosening his guests up.

"Interesting," Daire said to Murstyn, who was describing some new laws he'd enact. "Tell me more?"

He did, and all of it overheard by the flock of papagae suddenly rustling in the decorative privacy hedging around the elves' table. They all bore the same markings as the one Gage had summoned and that Daire had taken over. So had he fooled the elves into thinking he'd sent it on its way, but replicated it, to use as witnesses? The birds' twittering suggested they had the gist, and Gage and Daire would testify too. But how would they get the villainous elves to justice?

"Trust me."

Gage hadn't meant to narrowcast his question and hadn't known Daire could tune in. Much less answer. "*I do. I do,*" he thought back.

"*We're catching lawbreakers, not getting hitched!*" Daire's laugh was clear in Gage's head. "*Calm your talons, griffin.*"

"*If you stop twitching your turned-up nose at me, pixie,*" Gage told him, his grin taking over his face.

Chapter Twenty-Three

Gage is here! He's come. He understood and, more crucially, felt the same as Daire did...about everything, Daire hoped, his heart thumping. Look at him, Daire the pixie, head over heels, heart-deep for another. Him, Daire the footloose, fancy-free...lonely pixie, who'd never believed anyone would want to be with him long-term.

Gage does. Gage understood him, all of him and liked it all. Was in like with it all. *No.* Daire made himself think the word. *Love.* It...bloomed, like the flowers did here under this sun, with the salt of the ocean in the air and the noise of the waves in the background. But...it would thrive once they were back home, wouldn't it? Whichever realm that was? Their lives were so different.

"*But our hearts aren't,*" Gage assured him.

"*I know,*" he replied, loving Gage all the more for understanding. But he had a job to do first. Look at him, developing a work ethic!

"So, once the Storm King's out of the way..." he prompted his fellow guests around the table.

"It's the rule of the Storm Cousins!" Jaxon declared, knocking his glass into Jaleb's.

"As it should have been from the start." Jaxon slammed his glass into Jaleb's and both vessels shattered.

"Imbeciles!" But Murstyn laughed.

"Not just the Storm King. Her consort?" Daire reminded the traitors, encouraging them to describe how Grlind would be dealt with. He flexed his fingers. Should he try an amplification charm, to make sure the papagae fluttering quietly in the hedge caught everything? Or not bother and just ask these idiots to speak louder? Gods. Were all elves this dim? Well, they'd probably never felt pixie power before. Daire tried to be kind.

He poured them all more pixie fizz and nodded. "That would be very kind of you, to get a trained death fiend in to handle Grlind's execution, yes," he agreed. "And if I can just finesse your plan to sell tickets there...maybe have attending the ceremony as a reward, instead? You don't want to cheapen the occasion with riff-raff."

"Reward...for those loyal to me?" Murstyn took a big sip of drink.

"It would bond you all. And you could give them a ribbon of honor for attending," Daire invented.

"Something to pass down the generations. And a good hold to have over them." Murstyn approved.

Daire sat back. "You've got it all locked up. Like that griffin will soon be when word spreads!" He faked a snigger.

"The way you turned on him. You've got a heart of stone," Murstyn said in admiration.

"Funny you should mention stone," Daire replied, his gaze on Gage who he saw understood that pretending to turn on him was part of the plan. "I collect the odd talisman and relic, and I acquired this from a fellow pixie."

He pulled a small shrunken head from his pouch and held it dangling by the hair.

"It's a doll's head?" Jaxon tried to focus on it.

"A gorgon's head." Daire swung it into Jaxon's face, then Jaleb's.

"Yeuuch." Jaleb pushed at it.

"Um, it's not much to look at," Daire agreed, swinging it in Murstyn's face, making him focus on it too. "But it turns those who gaze upon its face to stone!"

Nothing happened.

"I said, into stone!" Daire yelled louder.

Nothing happened a bit more.

"*Shit!* Don't say that goblin-fingered and ogre-toed Clove dicked me again!" Daire yelled. He shook the gorgon's head as hard as he could around the table's occupants, like it was a maraca.

Still nothing happened.

Daire was almost crying and could see Gage about to spring into action. No! This plan had to work! "Gazers into stone!" he demanded, his voice cracking.

Nothing happened again.

"Oh, fairies' foreskins and pixies' pudenda!" Daire cursed, banging his free hand down on the table.

Thunder crashed overhead and lightning rent the clear blue sky.

"Oh, what? It needed magic words to activate it, and *those* words? Do all Clove's charms need those words?"

Daire demanded. He held the gorgon's head in front of his face, its face turned outward, as if that would protect him from the roll of thunder that was so low it was almost on top of the table, and the lightning bolts striking down. He needn't have worried. While the storm had those at nearby tables diving for cover, it was localized to his.

"*Daire!*" Gage shouted, rushing over through the hailstones raining and icicles hurling down.

Lightning, so bright it hurt the eyes to see it, forked from above to where Daire and the elves sat. It split into three, one pure white strike for each elf. Thunder banged again and Murstyn, Jaxon and Jaleb were no more.

Well, not as they'd been. Gage reached Daire and they both stared at the three tiny, doll-sized versions of the elves, all standing up on their seats and squeaking their outrage.

"Ah." Daire's swallow was audible above the storm still raging. "I wonder if—"

"You got the wrong words?" Gage laughed.

"—that idiot elf talking about dolls messed it up!" Daire finished, stamping a foot as hard as Murstyn was.

"The storm's worsening," Gage pointed out of the dark clouds and bright flickers.

"And sort of...focusing?" Daire tried to understand what was happening now.

The clouds were just in front of them, billowing in a ball, one whose outline was illuminated by white light. It intensified to the darkest, brightest, loudest yet, and just as a bang that shook the entire area sounded, the clouds parted and a tall, regal, dark-haired elf stepped through.

"A storm portal?" Gage asked, pointing.

Whatever it was, it folded in on itself to vanish as if it had never been, leaving total silence behind. The elf walked forward.

"The Storm King!" Gage got on one knee.

"Queen? Jade?" Daire checked, getting down as well.

It was the same woman they'd met earlier, only no longer slightly dazed and confused. This one was commanding, imperious and merciless.

"You little shits!" she roared at her fellow elves.

"And pissed," Gage muttered.

Daire winced at the way she grabbed first one tiny being, then the next then the next to dangle them between the thumb and forefinger of one hand and used her other hand to prod and flick them, making them swing wildly. High-pitched squeaks, mainly petitions for mercy, filled the air, but Jade didn't stop.

"When I have my magic back, I'm going to kill you," she promised Murstyn. "Then reanimate you and kill you again. Every day. Twice daily if I'm feeling in the mood. Oh, I'm looking forward to that. And you two, my *dear* cousins…"

"Banished?" squeaked Jaxon, hope in his voice.

"Yes. To the Storm Palace dung-geon," Jade replied.

"Dung…geon…" Gage considered the name. "Is that kind of prison the kind I think it is?"

"Oh yeah." Daire was pale. "It fills up slowly, with… Well, the clue's in the name."

"I need a cage for these vermin. Could you please?" Jade asked suddenly, offering Daire a glass.

"Transform it? Of course." Well, he'd give it a go. The whimper Gage let out showed how fast and hard Daire had drawn on Gage's power. "Sorry," he whispered, concentrated, and from one second to the next a glass dolls' house, perfect in every detail, sat on the table.

"I could sell these!" Daire couldn't help exclaiming.

"Not as cages, pixie," Jade replied, dropping her ex-courtier and cousins down the chimney into the house.

"I think it's wonderful," Gage assured Daire. "And that you can conjure things."

"With your help." Daire smiled up at Gage. He reached up to stroke his face, smoothing the planes and angles beneath his palm. Gage trapped his hand and leaned in to kiss it. All three elves, standing peering at them, looked disgusted.

"Sorry," Gage whispered, realizing where they were. Who they were with.

"Oh, don't mind me." Jade looked at them both. "In fact, go ahead. And that's an order."

The elven leader had no dominion over either of them, but Daire was happy to obey. He peeped up at Gage through lowered eyelids and licked his bottom lip, then bit down on it.

Gage groaned and sank into the chair at his back, pulling Daire onto his lap. Daire didn't feel like sitting quietly, so he twisted to straddle Gage, looking deep into his bright blue eyes and spearing his fingers into his thick blond hair.

"Do feel free to kiss," Jade commented.

"Yes, please," Gage whispered. "In fact, do whatever you want to with me."

Arousal shot through Daire, as it always did when this big strong griffin showed that he trusted Daire enough to give himself over to him, to meet his needs with him. He leaned close, his mouth almost touching Gage's. "Whatever I want?"

Gage opened his mouth, perhaps to speak, but Daire pressed his lips to Gage's and kissed him, letting his hunger roam free. He pushed his tongue into Gage's mouth, relearning his taste. He'd never get enough of it. Gage moaned into the kiss and cupped Daire's nape, twining his fingers into Daire's curls.

So of course Daire had to shift, bringing his groin to Gage's. Oh, gods above, it felt so good to press, to rub and rut, to enjoy that delicious friction on his dick. Gage arched his neck, giving Daire more skin to love on. He licked and sucked on all he could reach, stoking his own hunger.

When he made his big strong griffin whimper, Daire felt like he'd won the lottery. Gage pressed into him, letting Daire feel his hardness, and knowing he was responsible for that sent even more heat to Daire's balls.

"Want you," Gage muttered, nuzzling a sweet spot beneath Daire's ear. He still had his hand in Daire's hair, keeping him close. "I've never felt like this with anyone before." He slid his free hand down Daire's back, to squeeze his ass. His fingers slipping beneath Daire's waistband ramped up Daire's breathing to panting.

Daire rose on his knees, intent on riding Gage to release, but a cough had him looking over his shoulder, to the waiter. And waitress. And receptionist. And...was that a maintenance worker? Those were certainly the hotel's doormen. "Ah. We'd better stop. I—"

"I see colors. Now I've met you. I see colors. Griffins don't, when they mature. We lose the ability. But I can again," Gage burst out, almost in one breath, his eyes on Daire's.

Daire blinked at Gage's outburst. "And...is the reason you see them with me sort of the same as me being able to access your raw griffin power?"

Gage nodded, looking shy. His big, solid soldier, shy!

"I see. Well, seems a fair exchange." Daire grinned, gave Gage another kiss and climbed off. Carefully.

"Wait." Gage stood too and reached for Daire's wrist. "Tell me one thing. You were bluffing about taking the bribe, and us living like princes in the elf kingdom, weren't you?"

"Babe!" Daire spread his hands wide. "Do trolls fart black gas?"

"I have no idea and I'm glad I don't," Gage replied, his forehead creased.

"Well, stick with me and you'll find out." Daire winked.

"Before there's any investigation of trolls' asses, we have a conference to attend," Jade said. "And it's in the Pixies Lands, and you know what pixies are like."

"Sexy." Gage slapped Daire's ass.

"Like griffins." Daire slapped Gage's.

"You know, you two should think about doing this professionally," Jade commented, her head on one side. "Oh not the..." She mimed kissing and groping, something Daire had never expected to see a ruler doing. "Although..." She shrugged. "Yeah, people would pay coin for that too."

"Your Highness?" Gage asked, when Jade seemed lost in thought. "Do what?"

"Oh yes. Investigate things. Solve cases involving interspecies incidents. Matters where those involved would rather law enforcement — or publicity — wasn't a part of it. Together, you have a knack for it." With a regal nod, she swept on.

"Oh." Daire considered. "Like a PI agency? Interesting idea." It would be a way they could be together. And he knew a certain leprechaun with a taste for adventure who would relish a change, and like to join them too...

"It would. And I want that. To make a life with you," Gage declared.

His words warmed Daire down to the tips of his pixie toes. "Could it work?" Daire tried to think. "We do both bring unique talents and abilities to the mix."

"We do." Gage nodded. "Griffin strength—"

"And pixie charm," Daire capped.

"Griffin power," Gage started.

"And pixie magic," Daire finished.

"Griffin organization."

"And pixie fun."

"In short, griffin days—" Gage held up a finger.

"And pixie nights." Daire winked.

Gage winked back.

Want to see more from this author? Here's a taster for you to enjoy!

Wild Ones: Destined Prize
Bailey Bradford

Excerpt

"What do I think? *I* think all this *X-Files* crap's nothing more than jerk-off fodder for teenage weirdos who never step foot out of their mommas' basements into the light of day. *That's* what I think. Oh, and I also think that *you've* gone from having a hard-on over it to getting your balls in a twist about it." Frank Bueller poked Sam Brannigan in the chest to punctuate his words.

Frank wasn't from much farther south than Casper, Wyoming, where he lived and worked, but he threw colorful 'southern' expressions around the *Herald*'s newsroom like X-rated confetti. Sam's theory was that Frank felt it was something a newsman had to do, and with the man dating from pre-internet days, no one had been able to check up on his background and call him out on it originally. Having gotten away with it, once he'd made editor, he'd run with it more.

"*Capisce*, Brannigan?" Frank, also not of Italian background, added.

"*Versteht.*" Having a German grandfather meant Sam could cobble bits of other languages together too. "Well, thanks for that."

Still staring hard at Sam, Frank blew air down his nostrils in true Frank 'The Bull' Bueller style. He turned to rap on the glass of his office window, signaling something to someone out into the bullpen, finishing his message by tapping on his wristwatch and holding up four fingers. "Look, Brannigan," he said.

"Don't tell me. Walk with you to the break room," Sam muttered and stood aside for Frank to lead the way.

He'd been prepared for this tactic even before he took up the job here almost two years ago. If Frank was pitched an idea that didn't grab him right away, he'd get the writer to go through it again while walking to the staff break room with him. A *Casper Herald* journalist had to be really fired up about his idea to sell it bigger and louder in public like that, which would convince Frank. If the journalist didn't want to make a public pitch, he'd drop it, which would save Frank the work of rejecting it.

"And if it's a yelling-down, explain and apologize for your screw-up and take your lumps right then and there in his office. Not the bullpen," Sam's father had also told him, having known Frank from their cub reporter days. Sam agreed with that. A public sales pitch was one thing, a public crucifixion another. Frank's approach to staff development and mentoring was old-school.

Which was why him not shoving open his office door and barreling through into the public arena surprised Sam. Instead, Frank took a quick solo walk around his office, coming to a stop before the *Herald*'s wall of fame and its photo of award-winning journalist A.L. Brannigan, in all his late-eighties high hair and oversized-eyeglasses glory.

At least Frank didn't cast a glance back at Sam, comparing and contrasting father and son. Sam's strawberry-blond hair, while longer on top than at the sides, was more messy from running his fingers through it than piled high with product, and his glasses more nerd-hipster—the jury was still out—than the red statement frames his father wore in the photo.

"You ain't totally happy here." Frank spun around to accuse Sam. "Is it business news in particular or the Oil City in general?"

Hell. Sam glanced down at the carpet, half expecting to see he was standing in a black circle—he'd been put on the spot. "I'm grateful you gave me a chance after I graduated," he started, wishing they *had* gone to the break room. He could use a glass of water right about now.

He knew he was lucky—not many grads went from college to a state's largest print newspaper, whose daily and Sunday circulation was over twenty thousand and to which the Wyoming Press Association annually awarded the cup for best large newspaper in the state.

"And true, settling in Wyoming was never on my wish-list growing up, but I'm fine here in Casper." It was a big enough city for him. "But while Casper's a regional center of banking and commerce, I don't intend to report business news forever, no."

"Hey, I already started you working on energy-related stories," Frank reminded him. He took another look at Alexander Brannigan. His photo didn't show the Pulitzer Prize for Excellence in Public Service Journalism he'd won for his investigation into a Wyoming utility company whose shady cartel practice had allowed them to overcharge their natural gas customers for years, but Frank's smile smacked of reminiscence for his former co-worker.

"We couldn't keep him here after that," he commented.

"So you got me. Hoping I'm a chip off the old block." Sam regretted the words as soon as they came out of his mouth.

"Yeah." Frank had probably never sugar-coated anything in his life. "Took you on as a favor. A legacy." He gave a bull-like snort at the idea. "And you're proving yourself. Your work ain't all bad. It needs less ripping to shreds every story."

"I— Thanks." Sam meant it. That was praise indeed. And true. He was learning a lot here. More than he'd learned at Syracuse, in many ways. Frank's dark-brown stare pinned him, demanding a fuller answer, so Sam tried to provide one. "Journalism...it's more than a family thing, a legacy, to me. I wouldn't have studied it if not." Well, he'd double majored in Creative Writing too, but there was no point bringing that up. He'd only get accused of having an 'itchy pen'.

Frank studied him for a few more seconds, then grunted. "So this is all about this cyber chatroom stuff you're nuts-deep in?"

"ShareAlike? It's a social news aggregation and discussion website network—" Sam started. Again. Only for Frank's upraised hand to cut him off. Again.

"You don't get enough of that virtual stuff with the computer edition?" Frank's scowl lowered his brows right down to his flared nostrils.

Sam did work a lot on the *Herald*'s online paper, pushing for more frequent updates and integrated video and other multimedia content. Someone had to. Maybe that could be his legacy to the *Herald*. Well, it wasn't as though he had a lot else to do. He was hardly out on a date every night. That scene had lacked any interest for him for a while now.

"These weirdo forums, with rednecks sighting Bigfoot and the wolfman, or whatever the latest craze is, after they get slung out of the bar..." Frank looked like he did when he ate spicy food. Sam expected him to rub his stomach to go along with the wince.

"So are the users heavy drinkers in rural communities who think they've seen something when they stagger out of the bar drunk, or teenage shut-ins who live in their mothers' basements?" Sam looped back to Frank's earlier pronouncement.

"Who the hell cares!" Frank sucked in a breath. "Nah, kid. You're doing okay work in this uranium mine story. I think it's gonna go big. Keep on that and keep pumping that environmentalist contact. Not these nutballs in chatrooms. You—"

"Sam!"

Both Sam and Frank whirled around at Tony LeDoux's urgent call from outside...at the same time as a tall, heavy-set guy shouldered Frank's door open and barged in, more furious than even Frank on a Monday morning. He stopped on seeing Sam.

"Just the lying piece of crap I'm here to complain to your boss about!" he barked, squaring up to Sam.

"Frank Bueller, John Keef from Cheyenne, CEO of Logistics Transportation Inc.," Sam said over his shoulder to Frank. Stubborn, he didn't step aside for Keef, and so staggered a little when the guy shoved him aside to round on Frank.

"And he's hella mad and hella strong," Sam's partner, Tony, added from the doorway.

"What's this about, Keef?" Frank didn't back down either. He also didn't look in the least bit fazed.

"This piece of shit here wrote that bunch of lies about my drivers taking goddamn pills to stay awake and that I knew about it!" Keef yelled, gesticulating at Sam. "That I was okay with it—that I fucking *encouraged* it!"

"Mr. Keef's logistics firm transports overweight and outsized components used in the wind power industry, you remember," Sam filled Frank in. Not that there was any need, with the boss' memory for details of stories, current and past. Frank regularly forgot his wife's and kids' birthdays and his own wedding anniversary, but never any specifics of stories.

"Oh yeah. They take the windmill blades to the landfill." Frank nodded.

"Bueller, I'm here to tell you that if one of my employees —"

"Several," Sam interrupted the CEO, using a fake cough to do so.

" — pops pills, I don't know anything about it. That's what I'm here about — I don't give a crap about the blades," Keef snarled.

"You don't? Then why are you cutting corners to meet the disposal targets?" Frank snapped back. "Like making your drivers work double shifts because you're not hiring enough men or got enough trucks?"

"*What?*" gasped Keef.

"What we ain't figured out yet is if it's because your business is in trouble or because you got greedy," Frank continued, the verbal equivalent of a one-two punch. "But we'll find out."

He raised his voice over Keef's strangled-sounding protests, his insistence that the lying bag of shit who wrote this garbage be fired before Logistics Transportation sued him, the editor *and* the paper if it dared print the story.

"Shout the odds all you like, big guy. I stand by my men. Which, heh, is more than you do. We gave you a chance by sending you the copy and requesting an interview — the story runs tomorrow," Frank announced.

Shouting "The hell it does!" Keef charged at Frank, who absorbed the impact and grabbed Keef in turn.

"See this? This is more like it!" Frank, mid-grapple, called over to Sam and Tony who were backing out of the door. "More like the old days! Proves this is the sort of stuff you should cover!" He paused to block a punch from his enraged opponent and land one in Keef's stomach. Both Sam and Tony winced. "*This* is the kind of story to get your nuts in a knot about!"

The two men's struggle had Keef knocking into the door, hard enough to slam it shut.

"Should we...?" Sam started to ask but subsided. No one else looked concerned, and Frank certainly hadn't.

"Guess we got Keef where it hurts." Tony cocked his head at the office. He raised his hand for a high-five, but when Sam didn't raise his, folded his arms instead. "You okay? Oh, The Bull shoot you down in flames?"

Sam didn't bother replying.

"Funny. You'd think he'd be more into it when all that UFO and crop circles shit is so retro." Tony cast a final look at Frank's office and made for his desk. "Guess you should move on, then. You know what it means when a guy gets obsessed with something that crazy to this degree?" He waited until a couple of their co-workers looked up. "Means he needs to get laid!"

"Like I told you, you're not really my type." Sam spoke even louder than Tony had. "But keep trying, and I might get desperate enough to take you up on it one day." He blew his partner a kiss.

"In your dreams." Tony blew him a raspberry in reply.

"Oh, you are. Wanna hear what I did to you?" Sam would never back down and usually wanted the last word. "It involved scented body oil, furry pink handcuffs and a rolled-up copy of the *Casper Herald*..."

"Oh, *Jesus*," Tony whimpered as Sam sat.

There was no malice in the exchanges he had with Tony, or any of the other writers, just a sense of familiarity, of having slipped into a role and playing it out, as if Sam had been there longer than two years. Most of the others had. Was he bored? He tried to follow the thought through. He liked the job, yeah. He enjoyed investigative journalism...but he liked features, and long pieces too.

A tiny beep sounded — the new message alert Sam had set up for the ShareAlike forum he visited. Okay, haunted. Maybe he was in a rut, and this was escapism — it had his heart beating quicker than the stories he chased for the *Herald*. He took discreet glances around and clicked onto the forum. Inaspectus had posted again! Sam scanned it. The guy, or woman, not only believed all the stories about the sightings in that one area but reiterated his own, the details the same.

Sam took off his glasses to rub his eyes. Did he really believe there was a wolfman — a beast on two legs, bipedal, as Inaspectus swore he'd seen it — loose in a small Wyoming town? Inaspectus claimed he'd been clawed by the mutant, and another user had a similar tale of a lucky escape from a 'were'. Sam didn't know why he was so into this crazy story...any more than he knew why he opened a map of the state to see where this place was. All he knew was that he was drawn there.

He looked up at two of the building's security guards hurrying onto the floor, just as Frank kicked his door open and elbowed his visitor out.

"Thanks, guys. Take out the trash," Frank instructed them. He handed the spluttering Keef over and pointed at Tony then Sam. "Write up the heated denial from the subject of the story, could ya? The piece is taking shape!"

"Sure, boss." Tony grinned.

Sam spoke before he knew he was going to. "Oh, hey, could I have a couple of days off?"

"Sure!" Spreading his hands, Frank went to set his office to rights. Tony followed, glaring at Sam for having gotten in first.

Sam looked down at his mouse mat. A gag gift from a friend when he'd been packing to head to Wyoming, it said SAVE A HORSE, RIDE A COWBOY. Well, the big cities didn't have many of the latter, but he knew where there'd be some.

Out in ranching country, where all these weird sightings had been…and where he was planning to go for the long weekend he was taking.

To the small town of Britton, Fallon County.

About the Author

A native Texan, Bailey spends her days spinning stories around in her head, which has contributed to more than one incident of tripping over her own feet. Evenings are reserved for pounding away at the keyboard, as are early morning hours. Sleep? Doesn't happen much. Writing is too much fun, and there are too many characters bouncing about, tapping on Bailey's brain demanding to be let out.

Caffeine and chocolate are permanent fixtures in Bailey's office and are never far from hand at any given time. Removing either of those necessities from Bailey's presence can result in what is known as A Very, Very Scary Bailey and is not advised under any circumstances.

Bailey loves to hear from readers. You can find her contact information, website details and author profile page at https://www.pride-publishing.com

PUBLISHING

Sign up for our newsletter and find out about all our romance book releases, eBook sales and promotions, sneak peeks and FREE romance books!